GREEN
WATER
GHOST

GREEN WATER GHOST

by
Glynn Marsh Alam

MEMENTO MORI MYSTERIES
New York

Memento Mori Mysteries
Published by
Avocet Press Inc
19 Paul Court, Pearl River, NY 10965
http://www.avocetpress.com
mysteries@avocetpress.com

AVOCET PRESS

This novel is a work of fiction and each character in it is fictional. No reference to any living person is intended or should be inferred.

Library of Congress Cataloging-in-Publication Data
Alam, Glynn Marsh, 1943-
Green water ghost : a Luanne Fogarty mystery / Glynn Marsh Alam.
p. cm.
ISBN 978-0-9725078-8-2
1. Fogarty, Luanne (Fictitious character)—Fiction. 2. Women detectives—Florida—Tallahassee Region—Fiction. 3. Halloween—Fiction. 4. Tallahassee Region (Fla.)—Fiction. I. Title.
PS3551.L213G74 2007
813'.54—dc22
2007025823

Printed in the USA
First Edition

Gratitudes to Larry Clark, Dick Wilder, and Doug Lyle for their wisdom in the fields of law enforcement, undertaking, and forensics.

Fear is not always a bump in the night. It's the rhythmic rattle of disembodied steps on a wet swamp floor when all other nature sounds go quiet. It's the brown stick in the yard that begins to crawl, the silent flash at the edge of your vision, the blowing leaves that chase you to your door. It's the chill on your neck when thunder shuts down the power, and you sit alone in a house at the edge of a primeval forest. Lightning strikes somewhere, flashing the room with phantom shadows. Stillness prevails. You hear raspy breaths cease somewhere in another room. And fear fills the silence.

CHAPTER ONE

"The legend tells us there is a volcano hole somewhere in this swamp. It spewed up burned rocks and smoked for months a long time ago. Indians tell stories of seeing the smoke rise above the cypress swamps in one long stream. They say when they got close, they could smell the burning stones." The old man tugged on his uniform collar and grinned at the crowd of walkers. The label sewn on his sleeve said *Folsom's Walking Tours*. "Now, them Indians were heathen, but in a Christian world, we'd say they smelled the brimstone of hell!" He laughed until his old voice broke into a spasm of coughs. Another label on his chest pocket read, Arnold Folsom.

"And just where is this volcanic hole?" A young man, a college student, swayed back and forth on his heavy walking boots. The first real cold spell of the season had hit the south, sending icy currents up from the muddy swamp floor onto the legs of the walking tour patrons.

"Nobody remembers these days." The guide grinned. He needed a shave. His stiff chin hairs gleamed white to match his thinning head hair in the winter sunlight. "Most say it's right around here somewhere, but can't nobody find it now."

"It just smoked out then?" asked the student.

"Like most volcanoes. But you know they don't always stay dormant." Folsom grinned again, showing stained teeth that liked

11

the taste of chewing tobacco. Thank goodness he didn't chew it on the tour.

"Do you believe this?" I moved close to my lover and fellow walker, Deputy Vernon Drake. Shoving my hand onto his arm, I poked him slightly for a answer.

"Sure, don't you?" He smiled down at me. "Luanne, chill."

"Won't be hard to do in this cold." I shoved my other hand in my jacket pocket.

The guide moved further into the thick, dead scrub. Around us, pine and oak trees blocked most of the sunlight but not the wind that shot wet cold clear through the jacket lining and skin cells. Winter in north Florida can be pretty bad sometimes. Cold enough to be called a hard freeze so sensitive plants have to be covered at night. Many a family had to spend their extra holiday money on new water systems when the cold got too bad. This year, the first hard freeze came early, the end of October.

Folsom coughed suddenly and spit a wad on the swamp floor. If the students cared, they didn't say anything. This old man must be the patriarch of the put-together walking tour. Surely he had sons and daughters who did the tours on better days.

The group of two college males and two females stood as close as they could behind the old guide. He didn't walk fast, but they wouldn't be discourteous enough to get in front of him. Too older couples, bundled for a blizzard, trailed behind the youth movement. Vernon and I took up the rear.

Both of us had heard this folk tale for years, and it was even recorded in books on the area. A volcano hole was supposed to exist in the swamp. It would smoke and shoot up burned lava rocks, so the legend went. We didn't believe it. An abundance of peat existed in the ground all over the swamp. When it caught fire, it smoldered and mixed with morning mists to set up a kind of swamp smog. That's what I was sure those old Indians had seen. Others were willing to go along with the volcano story. My neighbor, Pasquin, an octogenarian with a sense of humor that could fool you into thinking he was serious, said he was certain there was a volcano hole somewhere.

Vernon had a day off, and I had needed a break from correcting first year linguistic papers at the university. One of the college males on the tour, an anthropology major, had been in my cultural linguistics class a year ago. He nodded and smiled when we decided to join them on the walking tour.

"Now if you look just down this incline here," said the man, who must have been at least as old as Pasquin, my octogenarian neighbor, "you'll see a dark pile of dirt under a few leaves in the bottom. Just watch." He pushed his old bowed legs against the side of the incline and nearly slid into the "V" area of the bottom. I wondered how he'd get back up since both sides slanted sharply for about five feet. He approached the black mound and stopped. "Now most think this is just a pile of moldy dirt and if you hit it with your foot, it will crumble." He held up one gnarled finger, pointed back toward the mound, and shoved it with his booted toe. It didn't budge. It might look like dirt but it was solid rock—or maybe hardened dirt.

"You think this is lava rock?" One of the young men had followed him down to the "V" and knocked his toe against the hardened mass. "Looks like old stone to me." He smiled back up at his companions.

"Nobody knows," said the old man. "Just one place something strange has been found in these swamps."

"Anybody test it in a lab?" Another student, who looked as though he spent a lot of time bent over a microscope, stood at the top of the incline with his hands on his hips.

The old man shrugged and grinned. Instead of trudging back up the hill, he turned and walked down the "V" and further into the forest.

"You folks can slide down here with me, or just follow up on the rim of the bank." He spoke to those who had remained topside. "We'll all end up at the same spot."

"Where's he headed?" Vernon said, his face taking on a curious frown.

I shrugged. This part of the swamp wasn't my territory. It was in another county and sparsely populated. According to the ad in the paper, *Folsom Walking Tours* took you through "wonders of the swamps" so I figured we were headed for either more lava rock or some other impossible phenomenon.

"Why?" I asked. "Do you know this place?"

"There's an old graveyard down that way. I knew a deputy who investigated a few years back. Some young kid was found hanging on a tree right over some old graves."

"Murdered?"

"They weren't sure, and since the kid was black and hanging in an old slave cemetery, all the surrounding counties had the jitters."

"I don't remember that."

"Before you started helping in the department. And no diving involved. I was just a green deputy at the time."

"And was it a murder—a lynching?"

"No. Suicide. The kid left a note."

I didn't know how to respond. Was suicide prevalent among young black kids years ago? Now, it happens almost daily with the advent of drugs, sexual identity problems, hopeless families. It just seemed that after the civil rights movement, there should have been hope for kids like this.

"Did he give a reason?"

"Older brother and father died of cancer. He figured he'd follow."

The embankment we had been trodding gradually lowered until it was even with the ground where Folsom walked. When we had all caught up with him, he stopped and faced us.

"Now what you're going to see beyond these trees is a little bit of a clearing. If you look where you're walking, you'll see old gravestones turned over and broken. And if you look close, you'll see where people have scratched in names or pictures, even an X or two for those who couldn't write. No fancy engraving. These are markers for dead slaves. A few yards beyond the trees is an old Baptist church with a white graveyard fenced off behind it. Graves there are from the early 1800s to the present day. Weren't no slaves allowed to be buried there, so they took their dead to the woods behind the church and created their own."

He waved his hand and moved between two large oak trunks. The first thing the clearing did was allow a cold wind to blow straight into our faces. The college girls huddled against each other, as did the older couples. Vernon put one arm around my shoulder. But Folsom and the college males showed their bravura and began wandering the area, their eyes turned downward to look for the gravestones.

"Not much here," murmured one student. He kicked at a piece of rock that didn't seem a part of the scene. When the stone rolled over, it was dark on the underside.

"It's awfully cold," said a female.

"Yes, ma'am, we got a cold winter on us already," said Folsom who zipped up his jacket to his chin, jerked a baseball cap from his pocket and stuck it on his head. He coughed again. In old times, he'd be suspected of tuberculosis. I figured his problem came from too much chewing tobacco phlegm.

"Hi," said the student I recognized. "Remember me? Carl Mabry. I was in your linguistics class a couple semesters back." He stuck out his hand. I shook it with my gloved one.

"Yes, I remember you," I smiled.

"Hope you passed," teased Vernon. He introduced himself and shook Carl's hand.

"Yeah, I did." He smiled and turned to see his microscope friend head into the trees. "What are you looking for in there, Dalton?" he yelled.

"There are some markers in here," he yelled from among the pines. "Maybe the trees grew up later, after the burials."

Folsom had found a fallen trunk and sat down on it. He swiped at his mouth with a handkerchief. "Happened all around here," he said. "Nobody kept up a place like this."

The two girls had given up trying to stay warm and began looking for markers. When they found one, they leaned over and took turns trying to decipher the faded scratches. "Wish I had some paper and charcoal to do a scraping," said one.

"Yeah, but let's come back on a warmer day," said the other who stomped her feet as though dancing on graves would bring on the heat.

"Where did they find the kid who hanged himself?" I asked Vernon.

He nodded toward Folsom. "That's the tree trunk he's sitting on. It stood pretty much where it fell, a big old oak with some heavy branches. Deputies figured the kid had taken his rope into the tree, climbed out on the branch and hung himself by just falling off with the rope around his neck. Did the trick, all right."

Folsom heard us and patted the trunk. "Poor old fellow."

I wasn't sure if he meant the fallen tree or the dead kid.

The sun decided to grow dim at about three-thirty. This just made it colder, but at least the wind had stopped blowing. With nothing else to keep me warm, I wandered among the old stones, too. Their scratchings were now almost like weather streaks. The old pieces of metal and stone the slaves used to memorialize their loved ones, couldn't cut like the engraving tools bought in stores.

"Is there an old woman's slave house near here?" Carl asked.

"Used to be," said Folsom. "Might find a few pieces of old board and some stones or bricks where she built a fire." He stared up at the student, too tired to get up and show him the direction.

"It's true, then?" said one of the females. "Old slave women who could no longer work were put out into swamp shacks and told to fend for themselves?"

"Yep," said Folsom. "Lots of them did, too. Got to putting together swamp grasses and roots, ate fish out of the streams, killed some birds and squirrels. Lots of them old women knew how to make do."

"Wow!" said the girl. She may have been close to graduation, but she seemed a child who was seeing reality up against textbook cases.

"You folks seen enough?" He asked the older couples who had found places to sit on the rotting trunk.

Everyone had gathered in a circle, our breaths shooting out white mist whenever we spoke.

"Everyone ready?" Folsom stood up. His knees popped in the process.

"Where's Dalton?" asked Carl and he walked to the middle of the clearing. Facing the woods, he yelled, "Dalton Paige! Get your ass out here. We're leaving."

I glanced at the older couples and wondered how they would take the language. It didn't seem to phase them. They were trying to lift their collars over their ears for warmth.

The forest with its dilapidated graves sat quiet and still. Snakes would be underground in this cold. So would any black bears and Florida panthers, if any were left in this area. Not even dead leaves rustled. Until Dalton decided to burst from his jaunt into the woods.

His face had gone pale, and his mouth was open.

"Somebody's been digging back there." He sat down hard on the ground. "Shallow holes everywhere, and some fresh dirt."

Vernon, suddenly alert, let go of my shoulder and headed for Dalton.

"I'm a sheriff's deputy, son, what's the matter?" He had pulled out his badge and let both Carl and Dalton see it.

"In the woods. Check out the holes." Dalton gasped in breath until he pulled an asthma inhaler from his jacket. Taking a long inhale, he pointed in the direction where he had emerged.

"Stay here," said Vernon. He shifted his jacket and placed a hand on the holstered gun. From his pocket his pulled a tiny flashlight and disappeared into the woods.

I stood at the edge of the trees, but Dalton's classmates moved into the shadows. I could hear their footsteps on the dry leaves. Folsom stood next to me with his mouth open and shoulders drooped. It was a guide's nightmare to find something on a tour.

"Just animal diggings, I imagine," he said.

Somewhere in the darkness, an "oof!" sounded followed by silence. A female voice rang out, shooing hunkered down birds into a flurry of escape to the air.

"I can't get out of here!"

"Reena, where are you?" Another female voice called through the trees.

"Down here, damn it!"

"Help!" came the plea from her companion.

"Just stay still, both of you," said Vernon. Peering between tree trunks, I saw his pin light move toward the voice.

"She's this way!" Carl's voice called through the foliage.

"Damn kids," said Folsom. "They should have waited in the clearing."

The adults chuckled and wrapped their arms around their bodies. Foolish antics of the younger crowd were enough entertainment for them right now.

"Luanne! Can you make your way in here? Straight through. Look for the light."

Darkness was about to take over, and dead vines that grew from the trunks pulled at my clothes. I stepped on more than one grave marker before I saw Vernon's light. Voices led me to the group as it stood over a hole the size of a human torso. Reena, one of the female students, lay sideways in the hole, one leg tucked beneath her back. It wasn't a natural position, and I figured her leg was broken.

"It's oozing down here," she said. "And I can't feel my leg." She lifted muddy hands but decided against rubbing the leg with the debris. "I'm sitting on something."

"You're on your leg," said Carl. "I'm coming down there."

"Just a minute," said Vernon. "It's only about three feet deep. We might be able to pull her out. I don't want somebody else getting stuck in what might be the top of a sinkhole."

He sent Carl to Reena's back and told him to grab her under her arms. Vernon stood in front and lifted her thighs enough for Carl to pull. I waited until she was partially out of the hole, then grabbed her jacket at the waist and helped drag her onto higher ground.

Reena lifted herself on her elbows and stopped there, her face a frightened question.

"I can't move," she said. "I don't feel anything, and I can't move." She took in a deep breath and began to cry.

"You've done something to your leg, and maybe to your back," said Vernon. "You'll need to stay here until paramedics arrive."

CHAPTER TWO

Folsom had come part way into the woods. His lined face shook with fear and cold.

"My son said this might come in handy, but I can't remember how to use it," he said as he stared at his cell phone.

"Vernon has already called. Maybe you could get me to the church beyond the cemetery. Is there a manse nearby?"

"What you might call one. It's a little trailer in the woods that the church owns. Preacher might be there."

We turned and headed through the trees. The adults followed us without being told, cold and a bit grouchy at the inconvenience of having to rescue a young person who had dared to venture.

The manse was indeed a little trailer. More like a rounded piece of rusting tin stuck beneath a centuries old oak. Its moss and limbs scraped the top of the once-white structure whose tires were now cement blocks. Gullies ran beneath the trailer where rain water washed through the clearing in each downpour. I imagined a few buckets inside to catch more rain that came through the rusted roof. A propane tank sat at one end, not quite as rusty as the trailer. The only sign of humanity was the fresh pumpkin resting atop a cement block, possibly a candidate for a Halloween carving.

Folsom knocked on the flimsy door. His knuckles were white with cold, or maybe with fear of being sued.

"Yes?" said a voice in the shadows of a partially opened door. A waft of warm gas rushed through the slit.

"Reverend Jensen?" Folsom explained to him what had happened in the woods. "Do you have any room for us to warm ourselves until we can get back to the cars?"

The man jerked on the door. He finally pulled it open far enough to show his massive body, almost too tall for the little trailer. He had to be in his fifties, Scandinavian from the look of him. In spite of a bloated face and belly, he still had a pronounced bone structure.

"Oh, dear," his voice came out a deep baritone. "This place barely holds all of me. What if I open up the church for you?" He didn't wait for an answer. Pulling on a jacket, he fished around a wall for the keys and came down the wobbly steps. "Need to repair those. I'm going to end up on my face one day." He glanced toward the pumpkin and chuckled. "Lord has lots of work to do taking care of us."

He took the lead all six-and-a-half feet of him, and led us to the front of a tiny church. The brick steps were solid though most likely built by an amateur. They led to a double door, painted white like the rest of the building.

"I'll turn on the furnace. It takes nearly half an hour to really warm up, but if you stand near the vents, you won't freeze. Sure is cold for this part of the country," he said as he flipped the thermostat. "Hard freeze tonight. Have to remember to leave the taps dripping in the trailer."

"How come the congregation don't buy something new for you to live in?" asked Folsom. He rubbed his big hands together, making a raspy noise with their dryness.

"Takes money," said Jensen. "We prefer to keep the sanctuary in good shape. I'm warm, and that's about all I need." He turned and smiled at us, the sort of smile a kindly old priest might have made. But the eyes were hard, blue, cold.

I'd never been one to trust preachers, and however generous this man was, I didn't trust him. No matter, I told myself. I'm not here to be baptized.

I moved away from the man and the others who huddled over the big floor vent. The church pews shined with dusted and polished pine. Hymnals sat neatly in their pockets. The wooden floor had been waxed and the windows washed. No stained glass here. This was a Baptist church and such expenditures were too worldly. The pulpit matched the pews in wood and shininess. A huge Bible rested atop it, closed and covered with a dust cloth. Behind, too close it seemed, sat two rows of folding chairs for the choir. There was no tabernacle organ with tall gold pipes, only an individual one the size of a piano.

"Do you have much of a congregation out this far?" I asked.

"We manage to fill the church," Jensen said, joining me at the foot of the pulpit. "Simple people from farms around the area."

"Are there many farms around here?" I had lived in the adjoining county all my life and knew there used to be lots of corn and tobacco farmers here. I figured modernity with all its technology and need for housing space would have abolished the small farmer.

"A few. And they have children who live nearby and work in Tallahassee." Jensen's eyes stared down at me. I had the feeling of being honed in on by a robot sensor. "I fix up something for the holidays, for the kids, of course." The pumpkin in front of the manse was his "fix up" for Halloween. Did Baptists actually condone celebrating a pagan holiday?

My vision of an imposing giant at the pulpit, bellowing out in a lordly bass about iniquities performed by groveling humans, was interrupted by an even louder reminder of our mortality—

the ambulance siren.

Folsom reluctantly moved from the warm vent and followed me outside to the edge of the forest. We waved to the medics, who shoved aside tree limbs and stepped over dead logs to reach Reena. She lay in the same position, her head resting on someone's jacket.

After one of the medics got onto the ground with her and tested her reflexes, he called the ambulance to bring in the stretcher.

"She's twisted something in her spine, most likely," he said. "Let's hope it's temporary."

Reena began to cry, tears dripping off her face. "Will I be a cripple?"

The medic shook his head. "Just help us get you on the stretcher." He avoided a direct answer.

Two men stood at the top of the hole while two others grabbed Reena's legs and shoulders to lift her upward. Her winter clothes and twisted position proved awkward, and the one with the leg end was having trouble getting a grip.

"What is this?" He said as he hoisted her knees a few inches away from the damp earth. He stopped and stared down at his own hand. "Damn! It's a bone. I thought for a moment it was hers." He blurted it all out before he realized it wasn't part of his bedside training. "Sorry, ma'am." He looked toward Vernon.

"It was a buried bone," Vernon said, grabbing hold of the femur. "Maybe a thigh bone." He let his voice drift as he held it up to the light. "Must have been dragged out of the hole with the girl."

"Part of a slave body, I suppose," said Folsom. He stooped over and peered into the hole now that Reena had been moved to the stretcher. He stood up, slowly as though it pained him to move.

"No," said Vernon. "I've seen enough bones to know this just isn't that old."

Vernon placed it on the edge of the hole and, with a broken tree branch, poked in the dirt. Carl and Dalton had stayed behind while Reena's friend went to the ambulance with her. The four of us peered into the grave as Vernon unearthed two more bones, femurs like the first one.

"Has someone buried legs in one place?" asked Dalton. His eyes widened and he backed away, shocked at his own words.

Vernon looked up at me, and I thought his eyes agreed with what I suspected. Someone had cut up body parts and buried them around here.

"All I can say," said Vernon, "is that they aren't hundred-year-old bones." He looked down at the pile of dirt colored femurs, dropped the branch, and climbed out of the hole. Walking away from us, he once again pulled out his cell phone.

"I think we need to move from here," I said and made a motion for the two students to follow me out of the woods.

Carl and Dalton moved slowly away, trying not to trip on the undergrowth. I looked back at Vernon. "Who's coming?"

"Local sheriff," he said.

I moved from the trees, leaving Vernon to guard the scene for the lawmen who would come and cordon off the area. Back on the road, the medics lifted Reena into the ambulance, telling her friends to meet them at the hospital. It would be a long ride into the next county as there was no facility close to these woods.

Dalton began shaking, his hands unable to adjust his glasses without knocking them further off center. Carl paced, his hands in his pockets. Her classmate, Lily, had her cell phone to her ear, talking and walking as though one action could not happen without the other. Her voice took on the quality of a teenager telling the latest gossip of what happened at the party. When she finally hung up, she said, "I got her parents' number. They're really gonna love this." She dialed a long distance number.

Lily walked away from us. I could hear her giving information to the parents, her free hand waving in the air to give meaning to her words.

Again, the order of the universe was pierced by a siren. Two patrol cars pulled into the church yard. There was no paved lot, just a grassy surface with bare areas and a few oil spills from badly maintained engines. The right Reverend Jensen, himself, stood on the church steps, watching the parade of uniformed deputies head for the woods. The others, I assumed, stayed over the vent inside the church.

Vernon took one deputy into the woods, while the others put up yellow tape on the trees. When Vernon and the deputy emerged from the woods, he came toward me.

"He's asking for crime scene people from our office. They aren't equipped for this kind of thing in this county. Looks like I'll have to call it in." He gave a half-smile, and I knew it was something he wanted to be part of, a case of new bones and old graves. His curiosity would eat at him if he had to stay on the fringes. I smiled back, feeling exactly the same way.

"The county line is less than a mile away," said Vernon after he'd notified his boss, Sheriff's Detective Tony Amado, that he could be on the scene late into the night and maybe the next day. "When that kid hanged himself here years ago, we were part of the investigation because he lived in our county. No way they're going to keep us out for this one."

I sat on the church steps, holding my knees in my arms against the cold. The sky had grown dark, but the place shined in the eerie light of the giant halogens erected for the investigators. As the hours passed, a couple of television reporters showed up with camera men, but were rushed away by local deputies who stood in their lights and let the public know something had been found but they weren't sure what.

"Now that's really going to make them less interested," I said.

"I hope this won't last long," said Jensen who stood on the steps beside me. "And if I have to give a statement, when will that be?"

"Sorry, sir, but I've been around enough of these investigations to know it could be some time. Nothing moves fast if there is the possibility of murder."

"Murder?" His voice boomed into the unnatural blue light.

"A possibility," I said, not willing to discuss it further.

"I'll see to the others." He returned to the inside of the church.

I pulled the parka hood over my head and felt the warmth on my ears. If I didn't move, I would freeze. I walked to Vernon who had reappeared at the tape.

"Can you say anything?" I asked.

"Look," he said and pulled me away from the others. "More equipment is coming in tomorrow. They did some digging in some other depressions and found more bones."

"Femurs?"

He shrugged. "Tibias, small foot bones." He breathed out, his breath shining like ectoplasm in the lights. "We figure come daylight, we'll find skulls."

A deputy came toward me. "Miz Fogarty, can you join us in the church? We need to get statements and let those people go home."

Before we could reach the steps, a truck pulled up near the patrol cars and a man in his late forties bounded out, heading straight toward us.

"Is my father here?"

"Who are you?" asked the deputy.

"I'm Arnold Folsom, Jr.," he said. "My father was doing the tour today. I've been in Valdosta." His eyes widened in a face nearly as wrinkled as his father's. A full head of salt and pepper hair lay unruly on his head, shining blue in the halogens.

"Inside," the deputy nodded. "You own that land?"

He nodded. "Up to the tree line, of course. The cleared part belongs to the church." He stopped when he saw Jensen appear in the doorway. "It's not our church. We go to the Baptist down on the river."

Deputies came into the church and sat with various members of the walking tour. They took down statements on forms that would be typed up and spell-checked later in the night. A look of boredom on the officers' faces made it seem routine, a chore that had to be done. The best, of course, would know when something a bit off would be told.

I had given my own statement and had resorted to standing over the vent when I heard a voice from outside. It was angry, forceful.

"You can't come in here!" said the sheriff who had followed Vernon into the woods. His deputies stood around him, their stance like centuries who would shoot given any movement in their direction.

"You need to talk to me," said a black man, his eyes wide and frightened, but his carriage dignified enough to make a defined presence. "Those are our graves."

Back on the road, a group of three women and two men, with Bibles in their hands, stared at the crowd.

"Sir, the graves we're looking at don't belong to you. Not unless you've been killing people and piling them in there lately." The sheriff had both hands on his hips. When he yelled at the man, spit flew into the beams of light.

"Somebody is putting dead bodies in our graves?" The black man spoke in a forced whisper, his graying hair shining above the dark skin.

When no one answered, one of the ladies left her group and approached Jensen. I couldn't hear her words but her finger stabbed the air in several directions.

"You can't do this on his grounds," Jensen spoke loud enough for everyone to hear.

"Whose?" I asked as I came behind him.

"Folsom's." He pointed to the woods beyond the tree line. "They've been in a battle with him for years over that graveyard. They want it to be an historical site." He made a noise of disgust.

"Sacred grounds?" I said.

Their leader looked back at the woman, then turned toward the deputies who now stood like a wall. He stiffened as he glared at the barrier in front of him. "They are our dead!" he said.

"You must remove your people, sir," said the sheriff. "I'll get back to you tomorrow when we know more."

I moved close to Vernon. "He's said too much already," I whispered. "They'll go back and tell the world that dead people have been placed on top of their ancestor's graves. This will really hit the headlines tomorrow."

"And over there are the ones who'll tell the world," said Vernon, nodding toward the two reporters and their camera men who had not ventured far away.

As though on cue, the black man raised a fist toward the deputies. "Ghosts will rise now. They'll come green out of the woods like cold spears to strike us all dead for the insults we continue to hand them. You wait! It will happen." He backed off the property, the camera following him and filming every minute.

"I didn't know there were still disputes like this in these swamps," I said.

"You might not know a lot, woman," said Jensen in his lowest voice. "And don't think those ghosts he's talking about are spirits."

CHAPTER THREE

Statements done, the cold tour walkers were driven back to their cars on the other side of the woods. Vernon and I were weary to the bone.

"There's still time for a late dinner at Mama's Table, if we hurry," I said. I longed for the warmth, the smell of fried shrimp and grits, and companions who made me laugh.

We got a ride with a deputy to Vernon's car. He had parked it alongside the others who met for the walking tour at the edge of the Palmetto River. I longed for a boat. It would take us the shorter route down the river to Mama's Table, the best river cafe in the county, and run by a Mama who knew the swamp denizens and their gourmet preferences. It was a watering and feeding hole for local law enforcement, a place to discuss drowned criminals and the latest domestic hog that had turned feral. I smiled at this latest topic. When domestic hogs break out of their pens and return to the swamp, within days they grow tusks and hair and become ferocious. Too much of this, and the swamp becomes more dangerous than it already is with snakes, spiders, and gators. Stories of feral hogs growing to enormous sizes spread throughout the hidden houses and trailers that made up the abodes of lifelong human dwellers.

The patrol car stopped behind Vernon's car. In the distance, the sky was pale instead of pitch dark. A full moon lighted the tall cypress trees that stood in river water. In their branches, bare now from winter cold, black birds sat at attention in rows. I could imagine them sitting at a funeral for something unknown or unseen.

"Buzzards? Anhingas?" I asked.

"Vultures, just vultures," said the deputy who nodded and backed his car out of the dirt drive.

Vernon and I climbed the steps. Mama's Table was nearly empty except for a lone fisherman who ate from a tall pile of fish fillets on a platter. He sipped loudly from his beer mug, sitting it next to the two empty ones.

"Lordy, Luanne, I'm about to close the kitchen," said Mama. Her uniform skirt stretched tightly across wide hips. The support hose she wore with walking shoes made swishing noises as she gathered up dirty plates. "But, ya'll look pretty tired. What can I get you?"

"Anything fishy and hot," said Vernon. He motioned me to a booth away from the other diner.

"Pieces of stuff left," said Mama. She didn't wait for our agreement but went to the kitchen and shouted to someone to keep the oil hot.

"Vernon, is this going to turn into something really nasty?"

"Mama's food ain't never nasty," he said and broke into a grin.

"You know what I mean. Is this a mass murder case?"

"Who knows? Marshall Long is coming out tomorrow and will collect what he can for DNA and test for cut marks. Those bones became detached from the rest of the body somehow."

"Skulls with teeth are the best for DNA."

He nodded. "And I'm sure there'll be some out there somewhere."

Mama brought two empty dinner plates and a huge platter

piled with fried shrimp, grouper fillets, and mullet. She came back with a bowl of hot cheese grits and a basket of hush puppies. "Nice to have you come in late. You can eat up the leftovers." She moved to another table and grabbed a jar of her tartar sauce and another of store-bought seafood sauce. "You want tea or coffee?"

We opted for hot coffee and asked her to join us. She pulled up a chair and sat at the end of the booth, rubbing her knees and complaining of the pain. "Okay, what's going on over at the slave cemetery?"

"You know about it already?" said Vernon.

"Got all sorts coming in here talking about cop cars and ambulances and those white vans over there. Wasn't no big interest in the history of the area, I'll bet."

"Some people of the area thought we ought to leave it alone," I said.

"Yeah, I heard Preacher Billy Buchanan showed up." She laughed. "He's kinda the local color sort of element that keeps people interested in the area. He talks a line about saving history, but gets riled up, ranting about legends and such."

"He actually preaches in a Christian church?"

"Something like that," she shrugged. "I hear he puts a lot of emphasis on demons and bad spirits and stuff." She sipped her coffee. "Lots of what we call off-the-topic beliefs shot into his brand of Christianity."

"There's plenty of room for it, if you read that part of the Bible," I said.

"You go to a church around here?"

"Mama," I said. "I don't do church."

"She's going straight to hell," said Vernon.

"You're coming along with me, Brother!" I said.

"I sing in the Baptist choir sometimes, but this cafe fills up on a Sunday. I limit my attendance to Sunday nights mostly." Mama smiled.

"Do you know a big preacher named Jensen?" I asked.

"Heard tell of him. He's never come in here. Fishermen from down river say he's kinda hard to miss, being so tall and all." She leaned over the table. "Jensen and Buchanan, I hear, have this sort of respect-from-a-distance relationship. Could be something more like a Mexican stand-off."

I shoved the last shrimp into my mouth. Vernon took a grouper fillet in his fingers and dipped the end in the tartar sauce. The warm grits and hush puppies had filled us and chased the chill away. Mama rose slowly, her eyes closing briefly to the pain, and headed to the kitchen. She returned with banana pudding, hot from the cook's table.

"We make it the night before and chill it. You'll have to eat it warm."

The fresh banana and vanilla cream, warm and sweet, went down like something heaven sent. Mama made it from scratch. There was no bitter, store-bought aftertaste.

The night sky had no clouds, allowing any warm air to escape and the Canadian cold front to descend on the Sunshine State with a vengeance. Even Vernon's car heater couldn't keep up with the chills across my neck.

"You'll stay tonight?" I asked. Mostly I never asked because Vernon and I had become creatures of comfort for each other. Any day out would end up under my quilts in my refurbished swamp house.

"I've got to see to the plants and pipes," he said. He looked across at me, the moonlight showing mostly an outline. "Tomorrow for sure."

In my youth, I might have been angry and told him to go home and freeze for all I cared. But we had mellowed, knowing that some things had to done before carnal comforts. They would wait, and we'd be all the more grateful. I nodded. I would have to take care of things, too, before hitting a warm shower and the bed.

Vernon turned onto the road that led to my house. What used to be an uneven, deep rutted lane was now a scraped, gravel drive that crunched under the tires. It was still bumpy in places, but there was no longer any danger of losing the underpinnings. As he pulled into the front yard—which was really a heavy grove of trees that had dropped dead leaves everywhere—the sensor lights flashed on and surrounded the front of the house with brightness.

"Plato came out of the cold," said Vernon, pointing to my swamp hound who sat on the top step. He shivered and wagged his tail at the same time.

Plato and I stood inside the screen porch and watched Vernon back out of the drive. As soon as I unlocked the door, Plato hopped inside and curled up on his wicker bed. The heat came on and we were civilized again.

"You've eaten somewhere, haven't you?" I said and scratched his ears. "Pasquin's, maybe?"

When I checked the message machine, Pasquin confirmed that Plato had made an appearance at his house where the mutt dined on Cajun stew leftovers.

"You call me when you get in," said the deep, old man voice on the machine.

He may be in his eighties, but he still stayed up late at night, sometimes with his swamp mates. I dialed his number.

"You're sure late," he said. I could hear some Cajun music

playing on the CD player in the background. It had been my last year's Christmas present to him.

"Lots happened out there—other than the tour."

"I heard it on the television news tonight. Bones everywhere, they said."

"They don't know that," I sighed. "That's the rumor but no reporter got close to those graves."

"And you got a race thing going now?"

I groaned. Preacher Billy's group must have played up the insult to slave graves and turned it into a media opportunity.

"It's not racial. The bones aren't old ones. Somebody decided to dig holes and dump them in that area."

Pasquin chuckled. "Well, ma'am, you're getting a visitor." He stopped, allowing silence to fill the room.

"Don't tease me, old man. I'm tired and cold. What visitor?"

"Some lady from an organization called me. Said she had heard about you out here in the swamp and wants to talk to you about preservation."

"Why me and why call you?"

"Says she prefers the feminine touch and figured you'd have a better understanding of the situation." Pasquin's voice took on a mocking tone. "Said she understood we were friends and wanted to know where she could find you."

"Well, that's just fine! Sounds more like a reporter to me. How would anyone know I'm even involved in this?"

"Got you on camera. You're standing there big as life looking up at this tall guy and talking up a storm. Reporter in the background says 'Professor Luanne Fogarty seems involved again' and they stay on you for a while. Feeling famous about now?" He chuckled again.

"Did the woman give a name?"

"She did, and I remembered it. Olivia Jourdain," he used an exaggerated French pronunciation.

"Okay, go to bed. I'll take care of Miz Jourdain in the morning." I hesitated. "Is there anyone with you?"

"Just finishing the last of a little rum with good folks," he said, obviously turning toward his guests when his voice faded. I heard "here, here" in the background.

"Guess I'll have to stay awake in case some drunks get stuck in the river shallows."

It was an old joke with us. It had happened before when some of his guests attempted to travel home by boat and got hung up on cypress roots. That was in the summer. Rescuing them in this cold wasn't exactly what I wanted to do tonight.

And it was cold outside. I zipped up my jacket and headed for the carport. The styrofoam protectors for the outdoor faucets lay in the box where I'd left them last winter. It took a while to rummage about the tool box to find all three. Putting them on the faucets would be even harder in the dark. I held the flashlight under one arm and moved to the side of the house. The oleander bushes had grown too close and would come even closer in the spring. Making a note to get someone to trim them, I bent over and slipped the cover over the outdoor tap. Tightening the screw was tricky, and my fingers ached with cold before the thing was tight against the wall. Turning around, I heard a gust of wind in the woods beyond the bushes. But the clear night revealed nothing but a hovering mist that laced in and out of the tree trunks. Wind would have blown it away, at least temporarily. I hurried to the back of the house and slipped on the next tap cover. This one was harder and lower to the ground. Kneeling, I felt a nervous quiver behind my neck and kept turning back to see nothing but more mist in the woods. It would all settle to the forest floor and form frost before morning. The last cover took me to the faucet on the opposite side of the house. Here, the trees nearly backed up to the wall. It was a place where Plato would lie in the shade on a hot summer day. Tonight, it was pitch black, and the high oak branches blocked out any sky that might have been visible on the front. Before I could fit the device over the tap, I heard the crunch of dead forest leaves. I froze in a nervous way, finally jerking the flashlight around and shining it through the trees. The steps went quiet. "An animal would have run," I told myself. When nothing else sounded, I bent and attached the cover as best I could and walked back to the front porch. The heavy mist had nearly risen to the screen door. I shined the light about the porch before stepping inside and flipping the latch. Without waiting, I opened the door to the living room and slammed it behind me. Plato stood up and stared at me with his head tilted as though inquisitive. "He never barked," I said. He went to the front door, sniffed, then wagged his tail for me. "Old dog, I've got a case of the jitters."

Plato stretched, went off for a few laps of water, and flopped back on his bedding. His body heaved sighs as he went into doggy sleep. I headed upstairs for a hot soak in the tub. Even with a contented full stomach and the warm soapy water over my skin, I felt the cold mist around me. My mind raced through a graveyard, over a hundred-years-old, and thought about bones, lots of bones. I knew it was time to get out and dry off when I remembered several documentaries of murderers hacking up their victims in the bathtubs. Somehow the thought of a red blood mess ruined my own bubbles.

Downstairs, Plato began to wiggle and whine at the door. I had to walk onto the porch and unlatch the screen to let him out. My flannel gown wasn't doing the trick. It had to be in the twenties. The ground, where it was covered by tree shadows, had a thin crusty ice over the top. I waited for Plato. He often ran into the swamp and didn't come back for hours, but tonight he'd do his business and come running back for warm air.

"Green ghosts," I chuckled. My breath sent out a foggy line that resembled ectoplasm.

I stood on the porch, hugging myself and wiggling my toes in my fuzzy slippers. Gazing across the road toward the river, where a fine, cold mist rose from the surface, I could still see the shore and part of my landing, but not the part that jutted into the river.

Plato came running and stopped suddenly. He faced the river and barked, his body stiff and ready for a fight. I heard a splash like something hitting the water. A motor started up, sending cold birds off their frozen perches. I heard a scraping sound and finally the revving of a motor as it sped into the river.

I pushed on some running shoes without tying them and slipped a jacket over my gown. Hoping that I wouldn't have to dive in and rescue someone from the cold water, I crossed the road with Plato and stood on the wood landing. Plato put his nose in the air and bounced it around, trying to pick up a scent. The object of his barking had left in the boat, but something had hit the water.

Leaning over, I tried to see into the water around the landing. It was too dark, and the gathering mist kept me from seeing more than a few feet beyond the edge. I left the dock and picked up a flashlight from the house. Aiming it into the water, I spied the end of a handle about the size of a broom appearing at the surface.

By the time I retrieved a rake and pulled the handle toward me, I was freezing. Keeping a steady hand wasn't easy. Plato stood beside me, alert to the object I was pulling toward us when I grabbed the pole handle.

I pulled on it when I could get a good grip. Something was at the other end, but it gave way and came up with the pole.

It was wasn't a pole but a kind of harpoon. A bag had caught on its end, and I guessed had been knocked off that boat by accident. The bag weighed heavier as I brought it out of the water. Touching the outside, I felt nothing but hardness. Opening the top with dread of seeing a horror, I found stones. Big, old stones. Someone had collected stones from somewhere, put them in a bag, and carried them on a boat.

My head swam with possibilities—a collection of stones from the old grave site, a gardener's collection to put around a flower bed, rocks for a yard pond? The boater couldn't have been collecting them at my landing. There were no stones here. It had to be further back and away from the river. These stones were pourous, not slick like river rocks, and the Palmetto River had very few rocks anyway.

I cradled one of the stones. It was heavy enough for me to use both hands. Plato moved closer and sniffed over it. Evidently, he found nothing alarming and headed back to the edge of the river.

"They could have come from places where rocks are used to border graves," I said. I hugged the jacket around me and laughed at myself. It was probably something innocent. Some boater had to stop and do something to his motor, placed the pole with the hook and his bag of stones in an out of the way place where they fell off when he opened the throttle. He probably doesn't even know they aren't there anymore.

It was too cold to wonder anymore. I left the bag on the landing and returned to the warm sanctuary of my home.

Morning came way too early. The sun had just peeked through the oak limbs and began its descent into my bedroom when the phone rang.

"You're needed," said Vernon. "Bring the diving gear."

"Where are you?" I asked.

"In my house, in pajamas. I'm looking out at the frost all over the lawn, waiting for the coffee to brew. Marshall called me and said he thought we could look for stuff as well as anyone."

"Stuff?"

"The crime scene people did a survey of the area before they left last night. There's a deep stream running just beyond the graves. Our walking tour took us around the other side which is why we didn't see it. Marshall thinks there could be stuff—make that bones—under water."

"Can't he use the dive team?"

"Doesn't want to. Besides, I am part of it and you are, too, sometimes."

"It's too damn cold!"

"Warm suit, warm swim."

"You know better than that."

"You coming or not?"

There had never been a question, of course. I was paid as an adjunct diver and if my bosses wanted to lend me to another county, I would go. And there was the natural curiosity about this case. What the hell! A little frost never hurt anyone.

We agreed to meet at the church in an hour.

CHAPTER FOUR

A sweatshirt over a nightgown and clogs on bare feet aren't the way to withstand a twenty degree morning chill. The boat and its stones had haunted my sleep, and I had resolved to go back as soon as the sun hit the deck. I'd have to hurry in order to make the diving assignment on time. My shoes hit the wooden landing like somebody clubbing a running lizard. The water next to the landing sent up misty vapors into the frigid air. There were no boats on the river this morning. Maybe a few diehard fishermen would be out there, but they'd be lost in the fog. Plato followed me and got bored with a further sniffing. Where I stood on the landing was clear. Anyone sitting in a boat on the river could see me, but I couldn't see them.

In the past when someone, an unwelcome someone, used my landing without asking, it was for purposes not exactly above the law. Mostly, it was to spy on me to see what I might be doing about a pending case. That same kind of paranoia crept back when I couldn't find the bag of stones. I had left it on the landing, and it was too heavy to be blown about by breezes, especially when there were none. The only answer was that someone had returned during the night and picked up the bag along with the pole hook.

My entire body shivered as I headed back into the house, Plato shoving against my leg to get inside first. He shook himself as

42

though wet. He wagged his tail a couple of times and headed for his bedding.

I put a store-bought log on the fire grate, lit the edges, and closed the screen. It would heat up the immediate area for about three hours. Central heat was kicking on often now, a world of difference from the hot, humid days of a north Florida summer. I put on coffee to brew and headed upstairs for a shower. It was habit, a routine that got me awake and alert every morning. It didn't make much sense this morning as I would be jumping into cold water fairly soon.

When I came downstairs, dressed in a bathing suit covered by jeans and a heavy sweater, Plato had moved near the hearth to soak up the heat from the burning log. I shoved his bedding near him. He roused his head and plopped down again.

"Such is a dog's life," I said. I scratched his ears a bit and told him to hold down the fort. Anyone coming within a few yards would get the growl and bark of a mad animal. I headed out the door, pulled my scuba gear from storage, and loaded up the Honda.

"I had them bring the wagon," said Vernon, already in his diving suit. "Get in and I'll show you what we have to dive in." He grinned, and I cringed.

"You found a hot pool, heated by volcanic rocks?"

"You wish," he said. "Back where we began the walking tour, if you turn to the left instead of going straight, you'll see an old path. The fact that it's still visible means someone walks on it now and then. Scene techs followed it and found evidence of fresh digging in spots. They'll check the land spots but they want to rule out anything in the pond."

"Pond? As in stagnant, holding pond water?" I said. Knowing this might not be pleasant, added to the cold.

"Yeah, green algae and all."

Vernon parked the trailer as far into the wooded area as he could. I went inside and changed my jeans for the wet suit and scuba tank. This suit had a hood, and I was grateful for it when I saw the top of the pond.

"It's covered in algae," I said. "Shouldn't the cold take it off for the winter?" Vernon stood beside me, ready for the plunge.

"Takes more than just one little cold spell to kill off the food for that stuff." He smiled and winked at me.

Behind our trailer, a marked patrol car pulled up and deposited three deputies and Marshall Long.

"Oh, colorful dive today," Marshall shouted, his ample stomach shaking with laughter at his own sarcasm. He tried to pull on a white lab coat over his bulky sweater. It wouldn't fit. "Forget it," he said and tossed the coat back into the car. "Where are the others?"

As though his question brought magic, a van appeared from the lane and parked next to the patrol unit. Scene techs already in white coats piled out and began pulling equipment from the back.

"Just what do you want us to look for?" I asked Marshall. He placed his bulk beside us, making footprints in the cold damp earth that bordered the pond.

"This was a holding pond once," he said, "put here for a project that was supposed to be built but never was. Nobody ever filled up the pond again."

"Nobody but the algae god," I added.

I leaned over and dropped my fins in front of me, but before I could push them on my feet, a voice arose from the woods on the other side of the pond.

"You're not going in there?"

Preacher Billy had emerged from the trees as quiet as a beetle, his followers—three of them—behind him. Each was dressed in a black overcoat and rubber boots. Bill, himself, wore a tie and white shirt that showed beneath the open coat.

"You'll have to clear out of here, sir," said one of the deputies who had a roll of yellow tape in one hand. "I'm fixing to tape off the area as part of a crime scene."

"Can't you see this is desecration of our ancestral graves?" he yelled, his face turned slightly skyward as though asking God for help.

"Your ancestors buried people in the pond?" asked the deputy. He had already begun wrapping the end of the tape around a tree.

"Before the pond, years and years ago," said Bill, trying not to raise his voice again.

"We're only looking for modern bones, sir," said the deputy, his sneer turning serious as he made his way toward Preacher Billy and the group that huddled closer to each other.

"You can't desecrate the past just to find recent bones!"

The deputy, nervous at their nearness and running out of self control, said, "Just watch me."

"This place is haunted with the ghosts of miserable slaves, and they will not tolerate this," Preacher Bill turned toward the trees. As though on cue, birds flew into the sky, while one of the followers murmured, "Jesus Saves." At the same time, Bill raised his voice and called out, "May the angels put a curse on all of you!"

"Jesus and hexes," the deputy chuckled. "You got it both ways."

The other uniformed deputies, half of them black men, stood and watched the trade-offs between the deputy and Billy. Billy's followers watched from behind him.

Vernon turned to me. "You ready to dive into the algae? Maybe the place is haunted," he laughed, "and we're about to get slimed."

"There's a clear spot on the right," I said, while Marshall

groaned at Vernon's joke. "Let's go in there and maybe not get the stuff all over the tanks."

"You'd think it would die off in winter," said another deputy who had been assigned shoreline duty.

"Does, somewhat," said Vernon. "Come back and look at it in the summer. Thick as green molasses."

Our mission was to search the bottom for bones, and the bottom wasn't all that far down. These ponds were dug for runoff to ensure construction sites wouldn't cause flooding on the surrounding terrain. Without a constant running water source, they became green-topped pits for frogs and snakes, not to mention breeding places for mosquitoes. There might be the occasional alligator, but the water never provided enough food for the reptile to stay long. By far, the most prevalent occupier of a deserted holding pond was the bit of trash tossed there by the teens who parked and petted on late weekend nights. I was betting we'd find more beer bottles than bones.

We eased into the cold water, trying to avoid the algae. Underneath, it had put out feelers, tendrils that collected its food, creating a bizarre vegetable world dotted here and there with sunlight and other spots shrouded in shadows. The slight movement of the water created waves of snakelike strings that swayed in and out of the light from above. There were no pristine spring aquifers here. This was a manmade hole that held microorganisms to feed the green cover. Our swimming would stir things up, sending an odor of cold pond scum to surround the space where the deputy stood.

There was no need for a search grid in the small area. Vernon simply took one half and I the other. The bright sunlight meant we could keep each other in sight the entire time, even when we moved into the shadow of an overhanging tree.

I moved close to the bottom, a thick covering of mud where scraps of party animals left their mark. Besides beer cans, I found tattered coffee cups. The paper ones disintegrated eventually but the plastic ones would lie there forever for all I knew. When I spied a piece of yellow paper, I brushed my hand across the mud and came up with a hamburger wrapper. It had been partially stuffed inside a paper cup that hadn't even begun to fall apart. These were signs of a recent tossing. I pulled it from the mud and stuffed it into a net bag around my waist.

I moved up and down the pond floor, poking and brushing at anything that might be bone. I had begun at the center and moved to the west side, up and back the whole time. When I was near the bank, I hit the jackpot. One lone bone had poked itself above the mud. I pulled on it and found its knee joint attached. It didn't take a medical examiner to see, even in pond murkiness, that someone had hacked at this bone and missed the point. I moved to the surface, bone in hand and raised it above the water before my face hit air.

From that moment, things changed. Evidence bags took away the nearly two dozen more bones we found, until a dredging pump showed up on the back of a sheriff's department truck.

Vernon and I had finished our end of the deal, at least for now. We pulled ourselves from the pond, dripping with green slime and hoping we didn't pick up some rare organism to give us skin rashes for a month. The deputy still stood on the other side of the pond where Billy's group had come from the woods. He spoke into his phone. The protesters weren't there anymore.

Pulling off my fins and mask, I watched as deputies mulled about, pacing it seemed to me.

"Just who is in charge here?" I asked.

Vernon pulled his diving suit to his waist, dried with a towel and pulled a sweatshirt over his head. "I'm going to find out," he said and headed for one of the uniformed men.

I didn't wait. I hosed off some of the debris and headed inside the trailer where I changed into my jeans. The heavy sweat shirt material felt warm and cozy against my skin. I went to the patrol car and sat in the warmth of the sun rays that came through the wind shield.

Vernon returned, tucking his hands beneath his thighs when he sat in the driver's seat. "Damn cold out there!"

"And, what did you find out?"

"That's the man in charge," he said and pointed to the uniform deputy. "He's a homicide detective who wears a uniform."

I frowned at Vernon who shrugged. "Not our county, Luanne."

"Does he have a name?"

"Lieutenant Gerald Folsom," he said. "Grandson to Arnold Senior and son to Arnold Junior."

I sighed. "A family affair."

When the dredging pump arrived, it came with all sorts of personnel from out of the area. Lieutenant Folsom, trying to take command, had no idea how the thing worked but he made sure his permission was granted before any generator could be cranked.

If he thought he had risen to the seat of top authority, his ego got another crush when Detective Tony Amado arrived with his Sergeant, Loman the unbalanced, like a triumphant warrior. Both wore uniforms, something unusual for detectives, but they were headed to a civic luncheon awards ceremony. Tony might have just retrieved his from the cleaners, but Loman had part of the not-yet-eaten ceremonial casserole stuck to a few buttons across his belly. He had stepped in a puddle somewhere between getting out of the car and walking to the site, making the lower part of one pants leg look a different color from the other.

"We're a part of this now," said Tony as he stood beside Vernon. "Found some bones just across the county line in an old graveyard like this one."

"Old bones?"

"Don't look old to me."

Tony moved away without a word, his dark hair well combed and shining. All he needed was a cape and he'd pass for a godfather.

"Lieutenant Folsom?" Tony stuck out his hand and greeted the local man without a twitch of emotion as he produced his badge.

"We've met." Folsom's mouth twisted downward before moving into a half grin. It was an out ranking and both men knew it.

Before the two men could swallow their pride and discuss the bone find, a voice boomed from the edge of the woods.

"Maybe you can do something about this, Lieutenant Amado!" Reverend Billy shoved past the scene techs who yelled obscenities at the intrusion. "Nobody wants to respect the dead."

Tony turned toward the graying man, took a deep breath, and stuck out his hand to shake the Reverend's.

"I can assure you, sir, respect for the dead is in force. I even have an archeologist from the university coming to make sure the slave bones are not disturbed."

I sighed and moved to Tony's side. "Harry MacAllister, right?"

He nodded, took the Reverend by his arm and moved to a private section. He'd fill the man full of assurances, but his real reason for moving away was to avoid my questions. Harry, my old lover and one-time diving companion, was never far from the scene. Tony had trouble giving up his services even though Harry no longer dived. He was injured, physically and mentally, from an underwater cave bomb and never could handle the scuba tanks again. He became a risk for both himself and his diving companions. Even though we taught at the same university, our paths hadn't crossed for a while. He stayed with his dry bones on dry digs most of the time.

"Did I hear you say Harry MacAllister?" Vernon stood beside me.

"Tony's bringing him in as an authority on the slave bones." This wouldn't be pleasant. Vernon and Harry were civil to each other but one never really trusted the other. I was the wedge, the female in a primitive male dominance struggle. As far as I was concerned, Vernon had long ago won it, but he seemed to think he needed to maintain his position.

Vernon nodded and gazed toward Tony as he spoke with the Reverend.

"You know Reverend Billy? He's got this church in the woods, and it's his own unique verson of Christianity he spouts all the time. I think it's a combination of home-grown voodoo, Santaria, and some stuff from the Bible thrown in for a tax write-off. Once in a while, a member of his congregation will partake of 'bread and wine' with a substance in it and go off half-crazed in the woods. The good reverend has been investigated a couple of times for using intoxicants."

"Jail time?"

"Never could pin it on him. He said if anyone was ingesting—that's how he put it—they did it on their own." Vernon shrugged without taking his eyes off Tony. "I don't believe a word of it."

I slipped my hand into Vernon's. He turned and smiled at me, the assurance I needed that we were in this together no matter who Tony brought in to look at bones.

"Let's watch the dredging," he said.

We moved to the edge of the pond where pipes pulled water from the bone find and dumped it into a ditch near the road. Men with high rubber boots stood at the ending point, watching the grate over the end of the pipe. If anything got loose, it would be caught there and pulled out for analysis.

The dredging process would take hours, but it only took a few minutes to expose a part of the soft bank just above where I had found bones. Partially buried in the sandy dirt, but visible in the harsh light, the white of rounded bone took form. A tech in a white coat hurried to the area and pushed a yellow flag into the soft earth. He had to lie flat on his belly and reach over the bank to do it. Raising upward, he pressed on the side of the bank wall. His hand slipped, nearly toppling his upper body over the side. When another tech grabbed him, his hands scraped the side. As soon as he sat upright, the wall crumbled and three skull caps fell into the water.

"I guess we found the heads," I said.

CHAPTER FIVE

"There are holes here," said Marshall Long. "Who'd take the time to put parts of head bones inside holes they dug beneath the water line?"

"Ghoulish," said Reverend Billy, calm now and seeming to ignore his group near the forest edge. They huddled in a tight circle.

"Maybe they were put there before the water came into the pond," I said. "Perhaps right after the construction team dug the pond."

"That would make them a few years old—from the time of death," said Vernon. "Grinning Skull Pond. Like it?" He turned to me with a silly grin.

"Minus the grins right now," I said.

"Somebody needs to go to the turn off and put up yellow tape," said Tony. "We'll have to keep out the nosies along with the media."

"Too late," I said. "Half the congregation is sitting in the white graveyard, and at least two reporters have been here all night."

I stood at the tree-lined border between the ruins of the slave graveyard and the well-ordered modern cemetery. On a usual day, the cemetery sat with washed stones lined neatly across a well-mowed lawn. Today, the congregation sat on lawn chairs and blankets on the ground. Instead of shorts and sandals and picnic food, they bundled themselves in heavy sweaters and layers of socks.

Some drank hot coffee from thermoses; others preferred the covered cups from Starbucks. In spite of their invasion of the "rest in peace" area, they showed reverence by talking in low voices, even whispers at time, as though the dead might hear and repeat the speculation.

Reverend Jensen looked perturbed at being unable to stop the surge of live humans sitting atop dead ones, but he made the most of the situation by passing among the graves with more hot coffee and reminders to stay off the mounds and slabs. People nodded and smiled and opened up their thermos tops for his brew.

"Pasquin would love this," I said as I surveyed the crowd.

"Probably could tell you some tales about the place, too," Vernon said. "That pumpkin hasn't got a face yet, but I'll bet it's laughing."

We watched as a patrol car dug ruts and headed for the end of the dirt road to block off entry with the scene tape.

"It won't work," Vernon said. "People will just climb under the tape or come through the woods by the church."

"Or maybe traipse through the tour trail like we did." I looked around at the what Tony called the 'nosies' and anyone else who happened to be at the scene. "Old Mr. Folsom isn't here, is he?"

"I got him answering some questions," said Tony as he moved to Vernon's side. "Can't turn him loose with these guys. His own grandson is head of the local operation, for heaven's sake."

Lieutenant Folsom strolled toward Tony, his chest stuck out and his hat resting atop his head. "So, we've found three skull tops and it looks like there might more holes in the side of that bank." He nodded toward the dredging operation. "What you got across the county line?" He didn't look at Tony, but positioned himself by his side, focusing on the holding pond. There would be no eye-to-eye contact today.

"Just some odd looking modern bones in an old graveyard," said Tony. He worked his jaw, the only sign of irritation. He stared at the same spot where Folsom stared. "Don't know much yet."

"I suppose FDLE will take all the bones to their lab?"

"That's why Marshall Long is here." Tony pursed his lips.

If Tony had any information, he wasn't giving it up to this man. To counteract, Folsom took two steps forward and turned to Vernon and me.

"You can go home, now," he said, "we won't need divers any longer."

Before anyone could move, Tony turned and stood directly behind the man. "We'll need Vernon. He's a deputy and knows the case." He nodded, his face nearly olive green with rage against having to share what he believed was his "right of bossdom."

"I'll shove off then," I said and winked at Vernon. He would end up being the calming force between these two. It would be a long case even if it was solved in a week.

I left my scuba gear with Vernon and walked toward the church. Reverend Jensen stood near the steps, watching the dredging and the men in white coats that were smeared with red from the clay earth.

"Miz Fogarty," he said and took my elbow. "I should go and visit that young lady who was hurt in the fall. Care to come along?"

It wasn't an invitation I'd ordinarily take, but I wanted to see just what had happened to Reena. "I'll drive," I said.

Jensen looked relieved. Behind his ratty trailer, there was an older model pickup truck. I figured that was his only transport, and I preferred my old Honda.

"You'll have to come all the way back here later," he said as he did his best to squeeze into the passenger seat. He gave up and pushed the seat as far back as it would go from a standing position. With that, his six-five frame fit snugly in the seat beside me.

"I don't mind. I'd like to see what progress they make today."

"Maybe you wouldn't mind stopping at the Mart on the way back. I need to buy several bags of candy." He didn't push for an answer, but I couldn't find a reason to say no. I shrugged.

The ride to the hospital in Tallahassee continued without a word. I didn't know what to say to the man, not a usual state for me. I'd been to Sunday School and church as a child, but never quite accepted any of the reasons to have faith in something invisible. It seemed they all wanted to tell you how to think and if you didn't think that way, they wanted to threaten you with damnation in the fire pits of inner earth. Reverend Jensen, so far, hadn't proved he was different. And, the title "Baptist Preacher" made him one of them in my head.

"We're having a fish fry Wednesday night," he said, out of the blue and causing me to jump. "You're welcome to come. It's free but we are asking for donations."

"That's Halloween. Won't your kids be out trick-or-treating?"

He shook his head. "We're trying to discourage that. Too much trouble out there, too much temptation." He sighed. "Lots of places have their own parties now. Besides, it helps the church fund."

"What is the church funding?"

He looked at me, then turned back to the road in front. "We have bills, things that need repair."

"Like a new manse?"

"That's one," he nodded. "You see how I live."

"Why live out here? Why not get an apartment in town somewhere? There are plenty of preachers who don't live on church property." I was guessing here. I didn't know that many preachers.

"It's better with ours being so far away from neighbors. I can keep an eye out."

I glanced at him. "You're around day and night?"

He nodded again, still watching the road in front. "Yes. Unless I have an errand to run or someone to visit."

"Then you may have seen something, I mean someone, put things into the holding pond?"

He shrugged. "Not a thing. Not a sound. I've already told the sheriff. Whoever did that, picked his times."

"Anyone in your congregation ever take up scuba diving?" I figured if the water was already there and bones had been placed in niches, it would require underwater work.

"Not that I know of," he shrugged again, his huge shoulders moving inside the little car like he had a motor inside him.

We went silent again. It was like riding in an elevator with one stranger beside you. You watch the floors but the corner of your eye watches that person. You don't dare say a word.

"I'll see if Vernon wants to go to the fish fry. We just might be there." I was grateful for reaching the paved highway where the Honda, low to the road, would do its roaring noise and make the silence more unnoticeable. At one point, I asked myself why this man made me uncomfortable. I had no answer.

"Do you know the young lady?" He asked.

"No. I know one of her classmates. He was my student."

"Anthropology?"

"Linguistics."

There was no comment, not even a question about what that subject entailed. Either he knew already or just wasn't all that interested.

Traffic picked up and so did traffic lights as we approached the city limits. Construction work debris made for uneasy maneuvering through detours. I dodged the roadblocks and flashing lights and finally returned to the last stretch.

"You never asked how I got to be a reverend at my church," Jensen said. "Most people are curious about that."

I didn't want to say what I felt, that preachers got jobs where they could and hoped the collection plate would buy more than forty loaves of bread. "Okay, how did you come by that job?"

"It's not a pretty story, at least not in the beginning."

I squeezed my eyes shut and regretted I'd fallen into the confessional trap. Here was a man who needed to talk and one who had found a captured female audience. I said nothing, glad that soon we'd be pulling into the hospital parking lot.

"I got into some trouble with the folks at my old church."

"And where was that?"

"Atlanta, on the outskirts. Not one of the big churches in town."

He let silence intrude again. He may have been embarrassed, but I got the feeling it was more for the drama.

"Some money went missing. They never did find it, but suspicion fell on me and some of the elders. I did my best to assure the congregation that I had no knowledge of the theft, but hard feelings didn't soften much. We mutually agreed that I should leave, and I got this assignment."

"Does your current congregation know this?"

He shook his head. "No action was ever taken. I didn't feel I needed to bring that laundry along."

I turned to him briefly. "Then why tell me?"

He looked back at me, his forehead wrinkled. "This business with the bones and the sheriff. I'll be questioned, along with others, I hope. He'll find out about Atlanta. I thought maybe I could speed up things and maybe keep it under the table a little longer."

I didn't respond. He was using me, wanting me to tell Vernon who would relay it to Tony and on up the line until his record was old news. No wonder the man settled for living in a shabby trailer next to a graveyard, I thought.

We sat in the parking lot space a moment before opening the doors to make our visit. Jensen turned to me once again.

"We're all haunted by our pasts, aren't we? Forgiveness is the only answer."

I nodded. My past hadn't said "Boo!" yet, but I knew plenty of people whose pasts had scared them right into oblivion.

"Forgiveness sometimes becomes license for a repeat," I said and bit my tongue.

"Not in my case," he said and opened his door. "There really isn't anything I've done—like taking church money—to need forgiveness. There won't be a repeat because it never happened in the first place."

Hamlet and his thoughts on protesting too much jumped into my brain, but I'd said enough. I slammed my door and led the way to the entrance.

We found Reena in tears. Dalton Paige, her colleague stood at her bedside, his eyes wide with the fear of not knowing what to do.

"You'll be okay," he said and made a slight gesture towards patting the side of the bed as though caressing sheets would pass a sympathetic current through to the patient. "The doctor says it's only a temporary numbness." He stopped and stared as I preceded Jensen into the room.

"Looks like you have a room to yourself," said Jensen in an attempt to accentuate the positive. The other bed was made up, waiting for some other soul who needed tending.

"They moved her out this morning," said Dalton. His information had come suddenly out of his mouth, something he realized as a mistake when Reena gasped.

"That woman was permanently paralyzed in a car accident," she said. "She'll be that way forever." She swiped at her eyes with the arm not attached to an IV.

"But you won't, Reena." Dalton leaned over to her.

"I could be," she said.

Jensen moved to the other side of her bed, introduced himself, and patted her upper arm. He motioned for me to come close and told her who I was in relation to the tour group.

"And Miz Fogarty is helping in the investigation with her diving abilities," he said, attempting to smile.

Over time I had dealt with people who were ill and found they fit either the shut-up-and-ignore-it kind to the I-need-to-talk victims. I took a chance on Reena being the latter.

"What exactly did the doctor tell you happened?" I asked.

Reena nodded, confirming that she was the tell-all type.

"He said I landed on my leg and back, causing terrible spasm and paralysis. I didn't break anything, or damage the spinal chord, but I could end up with permanent tingling, spasms, and weakness. I just have to rest and wait for the paralysis to ease up." She looked at me, her eyes wide and full of fear.

"And you will get over it," said Dalton.

"Where are your other companions?" I asked.

Dalton turned to me, an expression of relief on his face.

"Carl hasn't had a moment to come by yet, but he'll be here tonight. He's doing some heavy research work so he tells me."

"You aren't doing the same?"

"No, you see, he's doing more into interviewing people." He grinned. "I'm not." He gave a nervous laugh.

"And the other young lady?" asked Jensen.

"Lily is with Carl," said Dalton, his eyes darting toward Reena, who had leaned back on her stacked pillows with a resigned look of desperation.

"But all of you are in the same department?" I asked.

Dalton's head moved from Reena to me and back again, his glasses slipping down his nose with the momentum.

Jensen leaned toward Reena and placed both hands on her shoulders, a gesture that would have made me push him away. She didn't move, just stared up at him.

"If you don't mind, I'll say a little prayer."

Reena continued to stare, then glanced toward Dalton and me. When she looked back at the giant preacher, she nodded.

Jensen stood back and took hold of Reena's hand. With his other arm, he reached toward the sky. He turned his face upward and closed his eyes.

I looked toward Dalton who had broken into a sweat. I wondered what he was afraid of. He stared at the preacher, then lifted his head, searched the ceiling, and squeezed his eyes into a tight shut. The need to chuckle awoke somewhere in my belly, but I stifled it.

"Dear Lord, guide the doctors in their care for this dear girl, and place Your loving hand upon her spine. Give her the strength to endure and make the best of her accident until You grant the cure. Amen." He lowered his arm and patted Reena's hand again.

I watched Dalton open his eyes but take a little longer to lower his face. I felt something missing until I realized Jensen had not ended with the Trinity as most Christian preachers do. His was just a simple "Amen."

Reena's eyes widened when she opened them but she didn't say anything.

"Your parents," I said, "have been notified?"

"Carl called them," said Dalton. "They live in Miami and will be up here today."

Jensen and I left the hospital in silence. I wondered why the girl's parents weren't coming until today. With an accident like that, you'd think they'd be on a plane that very night.

"Warmed up a bit," said Jensen. "This will be one of those seasons when freezing turns to burning. We'll be in bathing suits by Halloween."

I stared at the huge man who had just raised his hand to the Lord in prayer. Bathing suits? Go figure.

CHAPTER SIX

The ride back to the church had been silent until my cell phone rang. It was the linguistics department secretary.

"A woman called. She needs to meet with you about something urgent she said."

"Is her name Olivia Jourdain?"

"Yes, you know about it then?"

"I've been warned. If she calls back, make an appointment for tomorrow morning."

Jensen looked towards me. "You know her?"

"Olivia Jourdain? No, I've been told she wants to see me about something."

"And I can guess what that might be." He nodded to himself. "She's got something to do with those black history preservation groups and has been coming around the church a lot. Wanted me to take her to the slave graveyard a couple of times. I just pointed. It's not my land and I don't want to upset the Folsom family."

"Do any of the Folsom men try to run you—or her—off the land?"

"Haven't seen that happen, but they've got some disdain for the preservationists. A little snide remark here and there."

I left Jensen at his church door and walked the few yards to my Honda. A few crime scene techs were still at the pond, but the dredgers had retreated to their cars, watching their machine and listening for anything that might go wrong.

Vernon and Tony were gone, back to the department, according to one of the techs. Folsom, the younger, was still there. He had been sitting in a patrol car but exited when we drove up.

"Miz Fogarty!" He called from the edge of the woods. "How is the girl?"

"The girl," I said with some sarcasm that the man didn't pick up, "will recover."

"Thankful for that," he said.

I'll bet you are! "Could I ask you something, sir?" I said, trying not to look too fragile.

He put his hands on his hips, spit out a seed or something, and nodded. I let him walk to me.

"Any idea how that hole got there? I'm talking about the one Reena fell into."

He shook his head before speaking. "Not a single idea. Place is wide open. Anybody could walk into the woods and start digging."

"Even find places to bury bones," I followed his nod with one of my own.

"Looks like he got stopped mid-dig on this one," he said.

I wanted to ask him but thought better of it. If Folsom knew anything, he would cage it. This was his land, and like the senior, he didn't want to be sued.

The wind began to blow a gust but not the kind that made you want to pull your jacket closer. It was almost tropical, coming in from the Gulf side.

"Warm weather coming back in," said Folsom. He had taken his stance of feet apart, hands on hips, and chest slightly puffed out. I guess it was supposed to intimidate females who asked questions. "We'll have clouds and lightning before you know it."

"No snow?" I tried to laugh, but Folsom just stared at me. I waved and headed back to my car.

The few straggling grave sitters picked up their cups off the gravestones and moved to their cars. Along the roadside, the reporters' car was still there, but the two must have wandered into the woods. I saw no sign of them.

By the time I drove back to my house in my own swamp, the sun had set. The wind still blew, sending dead leaves into the road, their undersides wet with mold. It was a silent movement, not the rustling dry one heard in more northern states. In one spot, a clump had blown into my driveway. When I got out and kicked it, a multitude of tiny brown frogs jumped about, scurrying to avoid any night bird that might find them tasty. Swamp law ruled here. Eat and run or be eaten.

"Thought you'd never get back here," came a gravel voice from the screened front porch. The light was turned off, but the sensors came on when I approached the steps.

"Dear God! Pasquin. You scared the religion right out of me." He sat in a rocker, his foot propped on a large flower pot that had yet to see a plant. I joined him in the other rocker.

"Religion? Since when?" He chuckled. "I don't recall you going into any sanctuary since my old cousin's funeral."

"No, but I've spent the afternoon with a preacher. Even listened to one of his very brief prayers."

"Yeah, your beau told me you'd run off with the minister."

"Vernon?"

He nodded. "Came by my place to give me this. Said he didn't trust leaving it under the door. I figured the walk down here would do me good." He pulled an envelope from his belt and passed it over to me.

"Not much to write on," I said as I realized it was an old envelope with nothing inside. Vernon had jotted a note and listed some items on the backside.

"Told him I could offer some paper, but he'd already had this wrote out and was in a hurry." Pasquin leaned back and rocked, his signal for telling me all he knew about this particular incident.

I switched on the porch light, causing Pasquin to groan. "Why not just go inside to read that," he said.

"Come on. Let's have some supper. It might be peanut butter, but…" He didn't let me finish.

"This old Cajun don't eat 'nut butter, ma'am. I'll rustle up something pretty good while you're reading that piece of paper."

I turned over the envelope:

> *Anything you can find on these at the univ?*
> *The 4 students?*
> *Maybe talk to black studies?*

He knew I'd understand. It wouldn't be official questioning as he would have to do, but more like snooping. I'd already planned to look into the students. And seeing Olivia Jourdain might lead me right into the Black Studies Department.

"This Olivia Jourdain," I said as I joined Pasquin in the kitchen. He knew me and my house too well. He had taken out eggs, sausage, peppers, and onions along with spices and was cooking up a large omelet in an iron skillet that required two hands and some muscle to lift. "I'm seeing her tomorrow morning."

"Not here? Funny. I got the impression she wanted to talk to you in privacy, like." He turned on another burner under another skillet and tossed in cubes of butter. "Got any light bread?"

"By light bread, I assume you mean white?"

He looked at me like I was a foolish child. Diet bread would not be in his vocabulary much less his cuisine. I pulled out a loaf from the fridge.

"Why keep it in there?"

"I'm single, Pasquin. If I leave it outside, it will mold before I can eat the entire loaf."

"Well, I know what'll cure that." He chuckled and refused to say anything more about my being single. He'd wanted me to marry Vernon and what he sometimes called propagate, but he'd given up lately. Certainly keeping white bread from molding wouldn't be enough of an argument.

"Hey, old man, how come you never propagated?"

"Probably did a few times," he laughed. "Just did it without benefit of that old Baptist preacher, not to mention the collared priest." He turned the omelet onto a platter, and pressed down on the four slices of white bread, now frying in butter. He took some sugar in his fingers and sprinkled it across the bread, then shook some cinnamon over that. The concoction shot out an odor that would send anyone's salivary glands into hunger mode.

"Where'd you learn to do that?"

"Propagate? Came naturally."

"Dirty old coot. I mean fry bread in butter, sugar, and cinnamon."

"Maybe from one of my lady propagators," he said and lifted the bread onto a plate. "Set the table, woman."

We sat at the table that had fed at least three generations of my family and ate something out of heaven. I had coffee brewing for afterwards.

"Tell me about the slave graveyards," I said. "Must be legends and even truths passed around this old swamp."

"Yep, sure are." Pasquin lifted a piece of omelet to his mouth and followed it with the sweet bread. He chewed a while before speaking again, but I could tell he was thinking. His mind was a gold mine for local data, better than any search engine on the computer.

"Not too many around here that anybody knows about now. Lots up in Alabama, maybe some in Georgia, but here they've either been plowed over and rest under new houses, or they get preserved in tiny little spots right in the middle of a development. There's one you can visit on the north side of Tallahassee. But probably many more as the old plantations were out that way."

"And the one on the Folsom property?"

Pasquin stopped to chuckle in remembrance of some odd event from long ago. "Say that's where the volcano is. Least that's what the old man wants you to think. Can't be, you know."

"Why not? No one knows where it is or even if it is."

"Indian legend put it more to the south of there. Supposed to be in a swamp that's full of hell and high water. Only when it gets good and dried off does the smoke appear."

"Yeah, when the peat moss on the swamp floor catches fire in a lightning storm." It happened in this area, sometimes making the peat smolder for days and causing an impenetrable fog.

"You said that, not me," he shrugged. "Legends tell of burning rocks flying up in the air."

"But no evidence has ever been found."

"None for ghosts, neither, but they are real." He shook his fork at me. "I've seen evidence over the years and I'm more inclined to believe than not."

The idea was making me punchy, and I began to giggle. "Ghosts? You? Come on, old man. Snakes, rogue gators, even moths the size of an airplane, but ghosts?"

"You ever stand on the edge of a graveyard in the dead of night? Well, you should. Won't hear a single night animal or a frog chorus—nothing. And it ain't you they're keeping quiet for. Something's out there."

"Phooey! You're getting ready to scare some kids for Hallow-een."

He looked up and frowned. "Oh, it is that time of year, isn't it?"

"Okay, back to the graveyards."

"You ever see a slave marker? They got their own legends, if you call it that, kind of from African beliefs."

"Not voodoo?"

"No, nothing like that. This is the idea of the spirit rising and what's got to be put where and how. They like flat surfaces with no grass and bordered in something. Round here, they used shells a lot. And what you think is a Christian cross is really a kind of nature thing. I can't explain it 'cause I never learned it. Neither can most people, but I'll bet somebody at your college can."

"I wonder if Preacher Billy knows any of that?"

"Doubt it. He's not college educated. Knows people pretty good, but not much on book learning." He looked up from the remnants of his omelet and pointed his fork at me. "Now be careful what you say tomorrow morning. I get the impression this Olivia person don't like old Billy too good."

Pasquin beat his belly like a drum and dropped off to sleep in one of the rockers after our supper. I'd made coffee, but we put ice in it as the weather really was turning. I rocked and dozed, too, until nearly midnight when he woke with a start.

"Got to get home," he said as he slapped the arms of his chair. "See your old hound came home."

I looked on the front steps to see Plato curled up. I never heard him arrive. "Did he know we were dozing and not want to disturb us?"

"That old dog knows lots, ma'am." He moved onto the steps and Plato rose to stretch himself. He licked Pasquin's hand and trotted off with him through the dark trees.

"Some dog, you are," I whispered softly, glad that he would accompany the old man on his walk through the night. It was feeding time for snakes and other animals of prey.

Mist had rolled in when the warm air and cold water vapor folded together. It tailed the old man and the dog into the swamp until darkness and the spirit fog engulfed them both.

CHAPTER SEVEN

Time sometimes stands still out here. There is no night prowler edging his way toward the foraging rat to strike, kill, and swallow. The frogs go below water and hush the croaking that seems incessant most of the evening hours. The screech owl closes its eyes and sits like a decoy on the oak branch. Even the river doesn't send its laps on shore with any force that would make a noise. The universe rests—but only for a short time. In the distance, a frenzied, high-pitched dog yelp sounded over and over, its sound trail moving rapidly through the trees in another direction.

"Plato?" I knew it was his yelp. It was the kind he made when he wanted to chase something away, like another dog or a possum.

I went inside and called Pasquin's house. He should have arrived by now, but no one picked up the phone before his answering machine clicked on. He used the prerecorded voice that came with the device. People his age weren't all that comfortable talking to another human on a phone, much less voicing instructions into a machine.

"I heard Plato giving chase. Call me the minute you get indoors." I put down the phone and waited. Waiting is forcing your own universe to suspend events. In the other universe out there, however, anything could be happening. I tried not to make scenarios in my head.

"This place is full of haints tonight," said Pasquin, out of breath when he phoned me. "That dog came alert two, three times before we got back here. Now he's done taken after something."

"You sound scared."

"When you don't recognize the sound, you're right to get scared," he said. "I heard steps, but they didn't sound like a deer or a human. And I sure know what a wild cat sounds like."

"Is someone out there?" I had pictures of night poachers looking for alligators or black bears or something illegal that required the cover of darkness. These were the most dangerous animals for a swamp dweller.

"Sure must have been. Hope that dog stays out of range."

I shuddered to think of how Plato had been wise enough to dodge alligators, a skill many other dogs wished they'd known when it was too late. He seemed to sense snakes and stay out of their striking range. I often teased him, telling him he'd become the Pasquin of the future, the wise old hound of the swamp. But a bullet was something else. A poacher would think nothing of turning around and blasting a dog into oblivion.

"When he returns, give me a call," I said and rang off. I almost left a porch light on for him in case he came back here, but decided against it. The sensor lights needed darkness to do their thing.

I spent the rest of my awake time trying to find out something about Olivia Jourdain. About the only thing I found was that she had a master's degree in history and was paid to be a liaison between the black history groups and the university. I dozed off until I heard a familiar thump on the screen door. Plato had returned no worse for the outing.

The weather was no longer cold in the morning. A familiar warm dampness gripped the still air. Boots would give way to sandals, ponchos to halters, for a while at least. The drive to the university required the windows to go down but no air conditioning.

I pulled into the lot outside the refurbished brick building that housed the linguistic faculty offices. It had seen better days. The trees around it had grown tall and were now depositing the green mold that happens in this mossy, damp part of the world. Not too many days from now, we'd be disturbed by the blasting sounds of a pressure washer. I pulled on the glass door's industrial steel handle, an addition made years after the building's erection.

"Luanne," a voice came from the shadows in the cool, dark lobby. "Nice to see you back."

I saw the Birkenstocks first. No need to focus on the face. It would be long and lined, topped by a partially bald head and stringy locks pulled back into a pony tail. Manny the Chair, as we had begun calling him a year or so back, had been the head of the department for too many moons to count. He was a fixture out of the past, still wearing the ratty jeans and letting his shirttail hang out. He shaved, it seemed, only every other day, wearing a stubble that didn't look in fashion even when it was. The hair and the gauntness, a product of a vegetarian diet, put him right out there with anti-war protesters. But, he lived up to his image. He was about the most peaceful person I knew.

"I didn't know I'd been away," I said. "Oh, you don't mean me?"

"This is Carl, an anthropology major who is consulting about his senior project," he said and turned toward a figure seated near a potted palm.

"Yes, we've met," I said. "He was in my class. Isn't this the plan where a project can be developed into a master's thesis in grad school?"

Manny smiled. "He's one of our finest students and smart to start planning this at an early date. Lots of students change topics too close to the date."

Carl leaned forward and saluted me. "I'm not quite sure what I want to do."

"You might want to do something in language, jargons, perhaps," said Manny.

"Jargons? What kind?" I asked.

"I'm looking into some professions and forensics really intrigues me." Carl stood up and offered me his chair.

"Let me get this straight. You want to stand around morgues and labs and listen to doctors and techs talk to each other." I privately wondered how many times he'd faint from the smell and sight of human innards.

"Yeah," he grinned.

"That's what has to be done, Carl," said Manny. "You'll have to write up a research plan and submit it along with your title and outline. Just remember, it won't be pleasant."

"Yeah," he said again. His grin took on a smirk.

"You may not smile so easily when you hear a constant buzz in a morgue and find out it's mountains of maggots feeding on human flesh."

He let out a laugh. "Don't try to scare me, Miz Fogarty. I know what it's like. I've already been hanging around the medical school here on campus."

I shrugged. Dealing with a senior project would be Manny's problem. I gave my good luck thumbs up and headed for my office. Thinking twice, I turned back and asked, "How is your friend, Reena?"

Carl shrugged and smiled. "Don't know. Haven't had time to pay a visit."

Manny looked from the student to me and back. He wouldn't ask. If it didn't involve the task at hand, he probably wasn't interested enough to make the effort. And, asking how someone was might imply that something bad had happened. Manny wouldn't want to hear it.

Inside the office area that I shared with other linguistic professors, things moved at their usual pace. Some spoke with students, others hurried off to or back from classes, and the odd person trying to write a book clicked the keys on a computer. It wasn't noisy, not a single radio played. These were thinkers who preferred listening to real language patterns.

I gathered the materials for my first class and stuffed them into a leather case. Leaving a sign on my door that said I'd be out of the office, I headed the few yards to Olivia Jourdain's headquarters.

"I'm Olivia Jourdain," said a commanding voice that came from a woman who stood close to six feet. "Please sit here." She offered me a soft leather chair near her desk. She wore a gray suit that looked expensive to me, and she wore it well. The white silk blouse, gold watch, and woven gold earrings finished off what was a work of fashion. Her hair, allowed to stay in its Afro, was clipped short to her head, allowing her almost regal features to display a beautiful face.

"I'm not sure how I can help you, Ms. Jourdain," I said, preferring the last name as her demeanor seemed to demand.

"I'm not asking for information about a crime scene or anything like that," she said, her voice taking on grace that was a long way from the rap music I could hear in the background. A group of students were collating stacks of papers in an open office. They moved to the rhythm of the rap as they moved along the table. Ms. Jourdain frowned and got up to close their door.

"That's good, because I wouldn't be able to discuss any police work," I said.

She sat down again and folded her hands on top of her desk. "I doubt you know this, but this office and the people I represent have a sort of on-going, shall we say, disagreement with the Reverend Billy crowd. We both want to preserve history, but our methods of conveying that are quite different." She looked down and gave a little smile. "His way, at times, is just too, too crude."

"Crude?"

"Loud, relying on emotion, invoking the Bible or some other religion, and sometimes getting into superstition, which makes all of us a bit stupid looking. We've asked him to stop showing up at places like the slave graveyard, but he's not going to do that."

"What is your method of preserving history?"

"The courts, if we have to go that far. We've been in discussions with the Folsom family for a while. They may have sold the plot of land to us, but when Reverend Billy came in, he got all this news media publicity, and the Folsoms added the graveyard to their walking tours."

"They can't be making much money off those tours."

"Pocket change, I would guess, but hoping for bigger and better. Billy feeds that."

"Nothing like evoking ghosts to attract a crowd," I said.

Ms. Jourdain nodded. "And now there are the new problems with the bones you've found." She stopped speaking for a moment as though in deep thought. "I was wondering if I could ask you to keep me apprised of anything I need to know, like when Billy or his people show up?"

"Ms. Jourdain, when I work on a case for the sheriff's department, whether in this county or on loan, I'm an officer of the law.
I couldn't discuss anything with you even if you thought you should
know it. Besides, the press is going to record Billy's visits. Wouldn't
it be better to contact them?"

She looked angry for a moment, showing a brow that could
cower an opponent in a second. Then she smiled. "I could, but
they like the battle and just as soon tell him about me as tell me
about him. It would be a game and a story for them."

I stood up and smiled back at her. "Then Ms. Jourdain, you'll
find ways to come out on top. You're intelligent and will make
more sense to the public, though Billy will be more colorful. Accentuate your positives." I stuck out my hand, and she eventually
shook it.

"May I call you from time to time?"

I shrugged and nodded. "Must run to class now."

I really didn't have to run. My class didn't begin for another
half hour, but I wanted out of the situation. Ms. Jourdain wanted
to use me as an informant, and since she could have placed her
own reporter on the scene, she probably wanted to know more
than when Billy paid a visit.

I sat on a bench outside the classroom building, waiting for
the class before me to leave. Anthropology students who ma-
jored in various specialties within that field sat on other benches
or on the grass, studying, sleeping, or in a couple of cases, testing
each other's hormonal levels. The weather was warm, but not hot
or humid as it would be in the summer. It wouldn't last long.
Another earlier-than-normal cold front was on its way from
Canada.

"Oh, hello!" A perky voice sounded from a few feet down that
path. Lily, Reena's friend, and Dalton, the other male student on

the tour strolled over to me.

"Hi," he said, his glasses making a slight slide down his nose. "You still working on that place out in the woods?"

I nodded. "Was that your first visit out there?"

He looked at Lily and turned back to me with a jerk of his neck. "Yeah. We heard about it when somebody mentioned an ad in the paper."

"The local paper?"

He looked at Lily again. "I guess," he said.

"And, Reena?" I aimed the question toward Lily.

"She'll be okay," she said with a whine. "She just wants to be okay right now, and that's not going to happen. The doctor said she didn't break anything."

"Still, it must be unnerving to not feel you limbs or not be able to move them."

"She can move them a little, and she's tingling something awful. It's all coming back if she'd just be patient." Lily put both hands on her hips as though scolding an absent Reena.

"What about her classes?"

"She might have to take some incompletes and do some making up, but it's not impossible!" Lily nearly yelled that last word. "Sorry, Miz Fogarty, but she's kind of like a baby right now."

I smiled and checked my watch. "She's sorry she hurt herself. No one likes to make painful mistakes like that." I nodded, took my case and entered the building.

Chomsky's *Syntactic Structures* and transformational grammar have the effect of glazing over the eyes of about a third of the students. Another third feels a light go on inside the head and their eyes reflect the glee. The last third try their best, but their eyes cry "Help!"

I stayed after and made appointments for office help, some of which I'd give and the others would be sent to a study clinic. This was a required course for majors, even for those who wanted to specialize in ethnic dialects or historical linguistics. I remembered Carl as one of the brighter students who caught on right away. It might not help much in morgue lingo, but at least he had a solid background.

Finishing up with my last class and appointments, I headed for the parking lot. The wind was blowing cooler now, and I figured we'd be in for a cold spell on Halloween. Unlocking my car, I heard the click of high heels headed my way.

"Miz Fogarty," Olivia Jourdain's voice called to me. "Could you wait a moment?"

I turned and leaned back against the side of the Honda. I never thought of myself as short until I stood looking up at this woman.

"I guess what I really need is to get into the scene a bit more." She seemed nervous, unable to say what she meant. "I mean if I'm going to argue with the Reverend Billy, I need to see him firsthand."

"You could try hanging around the site, but the sheriff's department is discouraging that." I looked at her and wondered how such a striking woman could ever do anything incognito. "Better yet, why not visit Billy's church, or Reverend Jensen's church?"

She frowned and turned to speak to the wind. "I just hate that." Turning back to me, she smiled, "Sorry. I don't know if you're religious or not, but I go to the Presbyterian church. I'm not comfortable where there is a lot of undue emotion paid to the subject at hand."

Talking like that, I was sure she would be an oddity in Billy's church. "I don't go to church at all unless it's for another reason than most people use. In other words, I go if I have to attach it to either a criminal or linguistic matter." I took a deep breath. "This appears to be one of those other matters, so you might want to show up. Take some people with you. Getting their perspective is good." I began to ask myself just what perspective she needed. "You want allies in your preservation work, right?"

"Yes, but I'd like for Billy to see it my way. It would work so much better, I'm sure."

I saw where her mind was. To deal with the councils and committees she wanted logical, even-toned discussion. She had the idea that Billy's emotional approach would make people turn and run. Depending who was on the committee, she might be right.

"You know, Reverend Jensen has invited all who want to come to a fish fry Halloween night. It's to keep the kids from trick-or-treating, which some think is dangerous. Why not come? You'll see the edges of the site, at least. And, who knows, you might get some help out of Jensen."

She looked around, a frown on her face, and finally took out a memo pad and wrote down the time. "I'm not sure if I will go, but I suppose he wants money from all who show up."

"Donations only," I said.

Olivia walked away from me, her mind preoccupied on breaking her mold. She had built her reputation, and this wasn't going to help it much. At least that's what I thought she was thinking. Her world was full of exuding the right image and not rocking the boat. Mine tended to tilt over the boat and dump mud in your face.

I drove the streets to the paved road that lead to my own paved lane to my swamp house. Before I got to the turnoff, a red sports car passed me at a tremendous speed. Arms waved out of both the driver and passenger sides along with whoops of pure road-conquering attitude. It disappeared around a bend and I didn't see it again.

The night eased upon my neck of the woods, bringing with it cool weather, some misty fog and a worn out Plato who needed a good brushing from his day in the forest. There were no messages. This worried me. I needed to hear from Vernon.

At nearly ten, he showed up with a light knock on the kitchen door which led to the backyard.

"Don't turn on the light," he said as he entered the kitchen. "I just hope no one saw me in your sensor lights."

I pulled him inside to the dining area where he couldn't be heard or seen.

"Something's up?"

"Looking for Nuggin Ires, who's probably roving the woods. He beat up a couple of guys at one of the bars down in Palmetto Springs. Knifed one pretty bad. We chased him and he headed this way. He sure must know the area. We can't find a trace."

Nuggin Ires had a reputation among the swamp people as one of the meanest drunks on the planet. The only ones who stayed around to cross him would be strangers to the area. His age was unknown but he could still fight like a full-fisted black bear.

Vernon checked my windows and gave Plato a pat on the head. "He'll stay around tonight?"

"You won't?"

"Sorry, love. I'll be awake on this for a long time. Unless we catch him, of course."

"Plato hasn't barked at anyone. Listen, will someone check on Pasquin?"

"I'm going there next. Old man like that would make a good hostage."

"Don't say that!"

If Pasquin were taken hostage it would be only after Nuggin had beat him senseless. He was the kind of drunk who respected no one's age, sex, or color.

I closed the door quietly behind Vernon and watched as he headed down the lane to Pasquin's. His gun was drawn.

CHAPTER EIGHT

After a fitful sleep, I awoke shivering. The house had cooled down considerably, and I pulled on a heavy robe. Halloween was going to be cold, and a good old-fashioned Southern fish fry would fit the season.

Plato wanted out as soon as he gulped down the canned food. I watched him take off through the trees, barking at nothing, or maybe announcing he was back.

I sat at the table in furry slippers and the warm robe, sipping coffee. The morning news said nothing about a drunk on the loose. I phoned Pasquin.

"You're all right then?"

"Was until you woke me up. Your man came by last night. Checked my locks. You got something to say. I need more sleep." His normal old man voice was deep in a gravel pit this morning.

"I'll pick you up tomorrow night, around six to go to a fish fry, okay?"

He was silent for a moment, then chuckled softly. "You don't want to go to a church event without an ah-com-pliss!"

"Why does the Cajun come out in you when you're ridiculing me?"

"Okay, okay. Six o'clock. It'll be cold. I'll have to find a jacket."

"You've got tons of them, even if they date back to the fifties."

I heard him laughing as he hung up the phone. I put the receiver down and sipped more hot coffee, nearly spilling it over the rim when the phone rang again.

"You want to come down to the lab?" It was Marshall Long. "Got something to show you about those bones you found—you and the girlie who fell into the hole."

"Has Tony been there?"

"He'll be here, too. Vernon says he'll drag in if he can. Been up all night trying to find a drunk."

"Then they didn't find Nuggin?"

"Nope, and you know what I think? He's sleeping it off on a dry leaf patch somewhere out in the swamp."

"How does he keep from getting bit by something?" I poured the rest of the coffee into the sink.

"What self-respecting snake wants to bite into a vein full of hundred proof?"

"I'll be there at ten," I said.

By the time I had showered and dressed, I realized I'd have to hurry at the lab to make a class in phonetics at one o'clock. Grabbing my case, I rushed out the door and ran right into Edwin who was coming onto the screen porch. Edwin was our local eccentric, the one who didn't wash much and lived with snakes both dead and alive. He rarely combed his hair and it stood straight up but for some reason never grew very long down the sides and back. He scratched it a lot. Most people who unexpectedly met him were scared of him. I knew he had a heart of gold and was one of Pasquin's most loyal friends.

"Ma'am," he said and bowed with a grin. "Pasquin sent me here to tell you something."

I was in a hurry but I knew this would be interesting and maybe even important. I sat in a rocker and offered the other one to him. He had left a bucket on the steps. I didn't have the courage to ask him what he was going to do with it.

"Okay, I'm listening."

"Well, the old man said something about you visiting that old slave grave site over by the church 'cross the county line."

"Yes," I nodded, wanting him to speak faster.

"I know another place like that only it's not too far from my place, and it's not near a church. Maybe was one there a long time ago, but not now."

"Does anyone else know about it?"

He shrugged, sending a whiff of dead animal skin my way. "Never saw anybody there. I don't go there much, but I was planning on going near there later this afternoon." He stopped talking and sat up straight. "Thought maybe you'd like to come along." He grinned, showing chewing tobacco stains and maybe even some fresh chaw remnants.

"If you can wait until maybe three o'clock. Sure." I smiled in return. I was curious to see if this place had also been invaded by more modern desecraters.

"Best if you can meet me behind my house. That's where we'll start walking."

I shuddered a bit inside. Edwin's backyard consisted of cages of live snakes, lines of hanging snake skins, and some coolers with, most likely, dead snakes waiting to become belts.

"I'll take the canoe and walk to your house from the river. Wait for me." I stood and held the door for him.

Edwin stumbled down the stairs and picked up his bucket. He had placed a long pole on the ground at the bottom of the stairs and there was tubing tied in a coil on the side of the bucket.

I waved as I drove off and wondered what would happen if this man crossed the path of a drunken Nuggin Ires. Of course,

Marshall was probably right. Nuggin would be sleeping it off in the woods right now.

The chill in the air seemed to enliven the people in their cars, who drove with the windows partially down instead of using the air conditioning. It was a welcome time in this part of the world after a summer of being able to feel the very air sit on your shoulders. The cars raced over the speed limit, and I followed, arriving at the crime scene lab just as Tony and his Sergeant Loman were getting out of an unmarked car.

"Luanne," Tony nodded, his only greeting and one always done with his guard up. He could never get over the fact that I was a female. He wouldn't tell me to leave, but he probably wanted me to ask permission. I never gave him that satisfaction.

"Did you find Nuggin?"

"Oh, you know about that?"

"I live out there, remember?"

"Didn't find him, but we will. He got lucky. The men he beat and stabbed are going to pull through."

Loman rocked on his feet and laughed. "All a bunch of drunk skunks. Ain't no beating or knifing going to damage those goods."

Tony shot him a glance. "Goods?"

"Well, it's a figure of speech." Loman's normally droopy eyes opened wide as a car pulled into the lot. "Vernon's here."

We entered the building together and took the elevator to Marshall's office. To reach his, we had to pass down a long narrow hall with a bank of windows on one side that revealed a woodsy outdoors and smaller windows on the other that looked into various kinds of labs. White coats, magnifying glasses, computers, and lots of bones. I'm sure tissue was there, too, but it was too small to be seen.

"Some people talk about a bone yard," said Marshall as he

turned on the swivel stool that you could only hear and not see beneath his girth. "I got a bone harvest in the pantry." He waved us toward another door that took us into a room where other techs were trying to match together bones into a skeleton.

"We could actually sing that old song about this bone connected to that bone. Still wouldn't make it any easier." He moved his large body between tables and stopped by one where he slipped on some latex gloves.

"Take this," he said, holding up a metal tray with dark earthy looking stuff. "This is bone material, but very, very old. Bet this fellow chopped a lot of cotton before they buried him in the swamp."

"Slave bones?" I asked.

"Likely. Not much preservation. The earth out there eats it all, flesh, hair, bones." He placed the tray back on the table, and moved through some equipment tables to a row of bones.

"Now these, if you see how white they are compared to the others, and intact." He held up a femur and turned it around for all to see. "Modern bones. And I mean late twentieth, maybe even later."

"How do you know that?" I asked.

"First clue is the condition. Elements haven't eaten away at the bone. Second is the embalming fluid."

"You can find that?" asked Tony.

"Bones have tiny blood vessels, and a good embalmer is going to saturate all the veins. True give-away that this man was buried after we started to embalm our dead." He replaced the femur on the table.

"But there is no flesh or clothing with these bones," said Loman.

"Now isn't that interesting?" Marshall picked up another bone and rubbed his finger down the side. "This was an old woman with osteoporosis."

"You can tell the sex?" Loman asked.

"I can once my techs have found a pelvic bone and labeled it." He pointed to a chart at the head of the table. "We've got parts of one man and two women here, all three on the aged side."

We stood silent, gazing at the bones and wondering why and how they got into the site.

"Could this be a case of funeral home fraud?" I asked. There had been a notorious case in Alabama where a funeral home just dumped the dead the forest and took the money for the funeral. The owner and his wife had made a bundle off reusing coffins.

"Could be," said Marshall, "but it seems an awful lot of work to dump them way out there. And," he put a moment of silence into his next speech. "Somebody went to the trouble of sawing and hacking."

No one knew what to say at this point. We just stared as another tech arranged a body in perfect form, announcing the first complete skeleton. "At least the large bones."

"And the skull caps?" I asked.

"Haven't gotten around to those yet," said Marshall. "Not too much use when we have no teeth for DNA."

Tony sighed. "Okay, Loman, get on the circuit and find out if they're any funeral homes or grave yards under suspicion of losing their customers—dead ones."

"Are you still working on the site we found?" I asked.

"Some," said Tony. "And we're watching the area."

"I've got an idea," I said. "Reverend Jensen is having a fish fry for Halloween, and we're all invited. Best to bring a donation, but it's free. Why don't we all head out there tomorrow night?"

"And Pasquin?" Vernon grinned, not waiting for an answer.

I sat across from Vernon in the Southern-style cafeteria. Its huge buffet of roast pork, fried chicken, white acre peas, sweet potatoes, and cornbread along with more expected fare like a salad bar filled the bellies of an assortment of travelers. Government workers drove here from their sterile state offices to eat the way their grandmother's fed them.

"If I fall asleep in my plate, pull me out and take me home," he said.

"Eat up and get home," I said. "I have a class to teach."

"Put me in that class right now and I'd embarrass you." He stroked his hand on the condensation of his iced tea glass and swiped the cold over his face.

"No Nuggin, I suppose?"

"No Nuggin nowhere," he said. "He'll turn up and get tossed into jail for a few days."

"That's all? After all those deputies who stayed up all night looking for him?"

"Of course, I wasn't out there the entire night. Some hour just before dawn I drifted back to the office to look up something."

He lifted the tea and drank nearly the entire glass.

"And are you planning on telling me what that was?" I watched him tear into a chicken leg.

"That old case of the kid who hanged himself in the woods all those years ago. It was inconclusive." He frowned.

"It's bothering you. Why?"

"Report said he didn't have a shirt on and there were scratches on his torso."

"There would have been scratches if he took off his shirt in the woods. And maybe it was easier to get the rope around his neck without the shirt."

"True, but deputies never found the shirt. If he had taken it off in the tree, it should have been up there or at least fallen to the ground."

"Maybe he went out there without one."

"It was cold that time of year, and it was night."

"Did you see a photograph of the torso?"

"Yeah. Kind of zig-zag scratches. Not deep. But there was also a photograph of the tree above him."

"Anything?"

"They found his books up there. His school books. That's where they found a note, too. Had that message about cancer that scared him."

"Maybe you should check to see if that fact was true—about his brother and father dying of cancer."

I checked my watch. I had thirty minutes to get to class. "Look. Go home and sleep. I've got something to do with Edwin this afternoon, but I'll meet you at your place tonight. Unless Tony is sending you out again."

"Nope. I've got a day off." He twirled his fork in his potatoes. "I guess you're going to haul me off to that fish fry tomorrow night?"

I smiled, kissed his bald head, and took off to my car at a trot.

Phonetics was another requirement for majors, and I rushed through the glottal stops and umlauts, telling the class that I wouldn't be available for appointments the rest of the day. On my rush to the parking lot, I encountered Manny. He had a long cotton bag filled with books.

"Only someone from the sixties would travel like that," I said.

"Take me back, please," he grinned. He wore a jacket over his jeans but his feet were still exposed in the ragged leather sandals.

"Ever think of teaching an anthropology course on that era?"

He stopped and grinned wider. "Now that's an idea!"

He stumbled into the building, and I got into the Honda and headed home.

Plato hadn't returned from his jungle jaunt when I arrived. I chunked my case on the dining table and ran upstairs to change into jeans, sweatshirt, and high boots. Just in case, I shoved my pistol into my jacket pocket.

Pushing the canoe from the shoreline, I piled in and took the oars. It moved swiftly and silently through the lily pads near shore and into the clear, cold river water beyond. The currents were with me, and I rowed easily past Pasquin's small dock. His boat was tied up, meaning he was at home. I rowed faster and maneuvered my way through hanging tree branches and patches of water hyacinth. Turning into a narrow lane, I was happy to be in a canoe and not a wider boat. I dragged it on shore and secured the oars to the bottom. From here, I took a worn path a few yards to a patched together house with a full front porch. That was where Edwin would sit in good weather and work on his belts and hats he made from snake skins. He wasn't on the porch today. I moved to the back yard and froze for a second when I heard the incessant rattling of snakes in their cages. Taking a deep breath and telling myself they were secure, I moved closer to Edwin.

"I'm here," I said softly.

"Yeah, I heard you drag your canoe on shore."

I gazed at him. "You heard me do that from back here?"

"Sure. I hear lots of things."

"Wow!" I said under my breath.

"Let me wash my hands." He went to an open faucet at the side of his house and let the water run on them, washing away any snake blood and remnants of skin. The rattlers kept up their noise.

"Doesn't this spook you?" I said, my skin beginning to crawl.

"That sound? No, makes me feel good. They're just being sensitive to our heat."

"Sensitive? I thought it was a warning before putting lethal poison into your system."

"Could do that, too." He acted as though he'd heard this for years. It didn't phase him. He picked up the bucket with its lid closed, attached the tubing, and grabbed the stick. "Let's go."

I followed him first onto a path that had seen some traffic. It soon faded away and we walked on dead leaves. Vines of varying scratchiness grabbed at our clothes, and lizards went scurrying into the brush from the sides of trees. It wasn't easy, and Edwin decided I needed to hold his pole to allow him to push aside some brush.

"Ever use a machete through here?" I asked.

"In the summer, when the brush is too thick." He held a briar branch for me.

I used his pole to push back a small bush that had grown near the path. "Edwin, this pole has prongs at the end."

"Yeah. Made it myself."

He didn't elaborate, but I didn't need anymore information. This was a snake stick, one he used to hold a live snake behind the neck while he picked him up and tossed him into a sack—or a bucket.

"You're on a snake hunt, aren't you?" I stopped for a moment.

"Yeah. Got a hole pretty close to the graves."

My heart beat rapidly and not from the walk. I patted my pocket to make sure I had the cell phone.

"Edwin, have you ever been bitten by one these critters?"

"Not by a dangerous one. Got bit by an oak snake once. They like to make you think they're mean." He chuckled as though talking about a child.

We came to a slight clearing no more than six feet wide. The other side was again heavy with trees. Edwin pointed toward a depression at the edge.

"Hole right there," he said and put down the bucket. He had fashioned a lid that opened half way and he flipped that part back. "You stand there with the pole." He pointed to a spot near him.

"Edwin, I'm not putting this pole on a snake head!"

"Not you. Just hand it to me when I say the word." He reached to the side of the bucket where a plastic container no bigger than a baby's bottle was attached. He then took the tubing off the side and uncoiled it. Unstopping the bottle, he poured a tiny bit of amber liquid into the tubing. "Gasoline." He said, carefully restopping the bottle.

He held one end of the tube and eased it into the hole. He was just as careful as any doctor at a digestive clinic. "Mustn't hurt him," he said.

"How do you know one is down there?" I gripped the pole, ever ready to hand it over and dash into the trees.

"Don't, but usually is. Snakes don't dig holes, just use some-body else's. It's cold today. He'll try to stay warm." He put his end of the tube to his ear and smiled. "He's there." When he had the tubing as far in as he wanted, he took the end, filled his cheeks with air and gave a strong puff into it. Finished, he pulled the tubing out again and began to coil it. "He won't like the fumes. Makes him dizzy."

And as if on cue, a big old rattle snake head crept from the hole. It seemed sluggish, and I was truly happy the gasoline had done its job. Edwin reached for the pole and I shoved it into his hand. Standing back, I watched him place the fork over the head, reach down and grab the snake behind the head, release the pole, and pull the entire four feet of reptile from the hole. Before the snake could catch a breath of fresh air, Edwin had him inside the bucket and the lid shut.

"I shook, but not from cold. "Are you going to get another one on this trip?"

"No. I never get more than one at a time. They eat rats and stuff. Upset the course of nature."

"Mustn't do that," I said under my breath. "Could we find some graves now?"

"We'll leave the bucket here. Just have to go in there." He pointed to a dark space between two large oaks and started walking. I took one look at the bucket and followed him.

"See there?" We had traveled only a few feet inside the tree growth when he stopped and pointed to some mounds. There were two old stones that looked as though they had been placed there, not at the heads of graves, but lying among leaves.

I walked closer, leaning over and seeing old scratching on one rock. It resembled the T shape of the old cosmos spiritual idea that slaves brought from Africa. I walked around a bit, through trees and pushed back some bushes. There were places here that seemed squared off and stones or shells bordered them. The stones were old and porous, looking a lot like the ones in the bag on my landing. Edwin was right, and someone in the field—like Harry MacAllister—was going to have a look at this place.

"Edwin, do you think you can bring someone back here, without capturing a snake?"

"Course," he grinned. "It's getting dark now."

"I mean later." I followed him and his bucket and stick back through the woods to his house.

"You want a cup of coffee?"

"Thanks, but I need to be off. And I'll be in touch."

He ignored me as he pulled out his latest catch and placed it into a cage. The gasoline had worn off and the tail joined in the chorus with the other cages.

CHAPTER NINE

Vernon lived alone on a lake. He had built his own house which had a long dock that led down to the lake edge. I found him sitting in a daze and watching the news.

"Just got up," he said and patted the space next to him on the couch. "Wonder where the storms are this year. Got too much algae growing in the lake."

"Such troubles," I said and curled up against his arm.

"You know what?" He laughed a little. "I've been ordered to go to that fish fry with you tomorrow night. Actually ordered."

"Tony?"

"Yeah. He'll be around, too, if he can get away. He says to wear jeans and stuff. No uniforms. He wants this to be a sort of family outing." He laughed out loud this time. "It'll be harder for Tony to do that than the rest of us."

"Pasquin's going, too. I invited him."

"Bet you have to pick him up."

I nodded. Vernon put his arm around me and we sat in silence, watching the news interview students about the next football game with its biggest rival. The comfort we both felt was welcome, and we had come to appreciate these moments almost as much as the mad passionate ones that came later. We had learned when and where to show affection. Only the deputies who had known us for a while or maybe heard gossip were aware we had a special relationship.

"Vernon. I've got to phone Harry MacAllister." I waited for him to say something, but he remained silent. Harry had once been my lover, a sore spot, but never one of argument. "Tony has called him in on this slave graveyard thing, and Edwin just led me to another one."

Vernon turned toward me and grinned. His wide grin and bright eyes had always let me know he trusted me, that Harry wouldn't have a chance in hell. "Call him, then. Be interesting to hear what he's got to say about things."

"You're not jealous?" I poked him in the side.

"Just stay out of his arms." Vernon poked me back and we both slid to the floor in a wrestling match.

"Oh, hell! I'm too tired for this," he said and rolled away from me. He spread his arms out and lay still.

"Rest, then," I said, "while I go speak to the expert on bones."

Harry wasn't an expert in the sense of a forensic tech, but he could tell you the sex, show you signs of trauma from arthritis to animal gnawing, and calculate the age. He had taken on more and more research in his department since he no longer used a scuba tank. Once Tony's most reliable diver, he rarely even took a dip in the university pool now.

"Tony said he called you in on this case," I said when he picked up the phone. He said he was happy to hear from me, but he sounded fatigued to me.

"Yeah. I've been out in those woods all day long. What a mess. Somebody mixed the modern bones in with old graves and bones that have turned to dust. Doesn't make much sense."

"Any speculation about funeral home fraud? Marshall said there was embalming fluid in the small vein tracks of the bones."

"He did? Then somebody could be digging up dead people."

"Tony's got Loman looking into cemeteries to see if anyone has gone missing or there has been any vandalism around graves. But, that's not why I called."

He chuckled in a evil way. "You want my body—alive and ready?"

"Don't flatter yourself, Harry. I want you to go with Edwin to what might be another slave grave site. I don't think anyone knows about it yet."

"Edwin? The snake man?"

"Yeah, that one. I was out there with him today. Way back in the swamp on what might be government owned land. I saw a couple of stones with things scratched on them."

"Describe the scratches."

"Circular with crossing bars inside and indistinguishable things in each quadrant. I left it all there. Didn't touch anything."

"If it really is from the slave times, it has been moved most likely."

"When will you go?"

"Maybe tomorrow. You get Edwin and come along yourself."

"Not Tony?"

"No need yet. I'll bring along some graduate students. If it really is a new find, they'll be delighted."

"Harry," I said, "what if you find more of the modern bones? Won't it then be a crime scene? Why have grad students where they shouldn't be?"

"Did you find any open holes or signs of digging? If not, then it's just a possible archeological site. If we find anything else, we'll call Tony on the spot."

We agreed to meet at my house the next day if Edwin was available. It would have to be late as I had classes to teach. Before ringing off, Harry made another pitch to be with me. He backed off when I told him I was using Vernon's house phone to make the call.

Edwin's television blared in the background when I called him. He seemed pleased and eager to be our guide the next day.

"You're going into the woods with Harry?" Vernon teased me. "Well, I'm just going to have to give you a night to remember so you won't forget I exist when you follow all that hair into the forest." He laughed and headed for the shower.

It was a known fact that Harry had a full head of salt and pepper hair while Vernon was bald. I had no trouble with bald.

While he showered, I made a dinner of fried mullet, grits, and slaw. It was a smaller version of what we'd get the next night at the fish fry. Only there, the cooking would be done in three large cauldrons—fish, hush puppies, grits. "Talk about 'bubble, bubble, toil, and trouble'," I said as I scooped the food onto plates.

We ate in the twilight. A fog had collected on the lake and was easing its way up the dock. Soon we wouldn't be able to see the water at all.

"Nice night for you to be here," he said, shoveling grits into his mouth.

"Always," I agreed. "Let's hope you don't get called out—please."

It was the bane of every deputies' mate. Get settled, in the mood, and boom! the phone rings and you're alone for the rest of the night.

"You'll come with me if I am called, right?"

I shook my head. "Sorry, I've got classes to teach and a trek to make into the woods before I pick up Pasquin and head for a fish fry at a church. You're on your own if that phone rings."

It didn't ring, and we pushed our middle-aged bodies into his king-size bed and swam circles around each other until we were like two creatures spent with a magical dust of afterglow. Vernon drifted into a deep slumber. I remember looking out the window and seeing mist undulate amongst the pines and oaks. It reminded me of children's tales of sweet ghosts of the South.

The next day, we were both off early. I had work to do in my office before class and some students who needed appointments. Making a run by my house, I grabbed some papers and rushed to the university.

By the end of classes, I had exhausted my intellectual acrobatics and looked forward to a long walk in the woods. On the way to my car, Carl Mabry stopped to ask if I planned to go to the fish fry.

"Yes. How did you know about it?"

"That preacher invited us, remember?" He grinned and nodded for his friend, Dalton, to join us. "We're both going."

"I'm not sure if I can," said Dalton and lowered his head.

"Sure, you can," said Carl and nudged him with his elbow.

"Will Lily come, too?" I asked.

"Probably," said Carl. "The four of us hang out together."

"I have to run," I said. "I'm going to a site with Dr. MacAllister."

"Yeah?" Carl's face took on a little boy expression. He seemed to be getting good at that. "Can we come along?"

"Not this time. It's his show. We're not even sure if the site is authentic." I gave a salute and opened the car door. As I pulled out of the lot, I noticed through the side mirror that both boys watched the car leave. They were standing next to a small red sports car like the one that had passed me like a rocket.

Traffic was thick because of construction, but I managed to pull a few weaves and tailgates and thought I'd be home in record time. Harry beat me to it. He was rocking on the front porch when I arrived.

"Good to see you, Luanne," he said and made a move to hug me.

"Right, Harry," I said and moved away. "Are you okay to ride in a canoe?"

"Of course," he hung his head a bit, embarrassed by his terror of diving that had driven him from exploring and mapping underwater cave routes. One jerk's attempt to kill us both with an underwater bomb had permanently unnerved him.

"How's the leg?"

"Still there. Some days are worse than others."

Harry's leg had been broken in that underwater event, but the doctors said it had completely and correctly healed. His limp was psychological.

"Give me a moment to change."

I ran inside and put on jeans and a sweatshirt, grabbed my jacket, with the pistol in the pocket, and headed for the carport where I kept the red canoe that Vernon had given me. It had been a peace offering after an argument about Harry and those words were emblazoned on the side near the front The irony that Harry would be riding in this canoe wasn't lost on me.

"Do you know Edwin?" I handed one oar to Harry who sat in the rear.

"Not well, but I've seen him around. Funny guy."

"Not exactly a comic. More like the swamp weirdo," I said and nodded for us to shove off and head for the middle of the river.

We rowed steadily. Harry kept up the pace, showing no fear of being on the water. We pulled the canoe onto shore at Edwin's dock.

"You ready to go again?" Edwin grinned as though he were the sought after celebrity.

"Yeah, but no snake hunt this time, promise?" I said.

Harry walked around the cages and tables in Edwin's back-yard. Live snakes shook their rattles in a nonstop rasping. He seemed fascinated.

Even though he left the bucket and tubing behind, Edwin took his hooked pole with him as he led us through the forest.

"Anyone else come back here?" Harry asked, holding back a sticky vine and brushing away a long legged black and white banana spider.

"Could be," Edwin shrugged. "I think I heard something one time. I was pulling a snake from a hole and turned around when I felt steps on the leaves. Soon as I held up that snake, those steps went running the other way." He chuckled, and I wasn't sure if he made it all up or someone had followed him out here.

We walked to the edge of the clearing. I spied the snake hole he had pulled the drunken rattler from the day before, and looked at Edwin to make sure he wasn't trying to find more holes.

"It's right beyond the clearing in those trees," he said, pointing in the direction we'd found the stones.

Inside the tree coverage, the ground had its familiar look of some kind of clearing done years ago. Harry kneeled to inspect the stone I had seen with its scratches. He bent over it with a tiny flashlight, carefully viewing the markings before he touched it.

"Eureka!" he said with a grin as he picked up the stone and rose to a squatting position. Holding it as thought it were Hamlet's skull, he said, "Not what you'd call old, at least not the etching." He revolved the stone in his hand. "The rock itself might be from that time, but not the marks on it."

"How can you tell?"

"Etching lines are too white. Looks as though someone knew the symbols of the old cosmos religion, but it's too much by the book and the dirt hasn't had time to settle." He put the rock inside a tote bag he had brought. "The area, maybe." He walked about, leaning over at times to brush some leaves or grass away. "Seems like the area has been flattened and bordered at one time. That's a sign. The slaves might have put items like shells and broken pottery to border the graves, even stones on top to keep the grass from growing if they could—but not these stones and not these shells." Bending over, he picked up an oyster shell. "Probably left from someone's Sunday dinner. Could be someone is perserving the area by following old traditions." He stood still and looked around him. "This would be a very old spot because there is no plantation or white church near. It's all swamp. They would have had to walk a few miles to bury their dead here, not to mention the modern folk who placed the markers."

The three of us stood still and imagined for a moment the desperation of a people who had to drag their dead into hostile swamps to find a place to bury them. Edwin put up his hand.

"I hear the leaves moving," he whispered.

I heard nothing, and Harry looked at me with a skeptical smile, but we both stayed quiet.

"Someone's out there." Edwin pointed to the side of the clearing.

Harry and I immediately moved to the edge of the trees and gazed into the semi-darkness. Something took off in a run.

"It has to be a deer, Edwin," said Harry.

Edwin was shaking his head. "No deer. It's a two footer. Dear has a four foot run."

I wasn't going to dispute his talent for knowing what he heard. He was born in this swamp and literally lived off it. I doubt he ever went deer hunting unless he needed the meat, but he'd know what one sounded like. Besides, anyone who could hear "leaves" moving underfoot, had pretty sharp ears.

"Let's look," I said and moved further into the forest.

"If anyone walked on these moldy leaves, he'd leave indentations," said Harry. He leaned over and shined his light on the area where we heard the scurrying.

"Some branches on this little tree appear to be freshly broken," I said as I followed Harry.

Edwin was slightly to my left. "Here, too," he said. "And look at the leaves."

He had indeed found shoe indentations—human and recent. Just behind them, the leaves were disturbed, their wet and moldy undersides stirred up and turned over as though someone turned on his heels and ran.

"Harry," I said. "I think we were being watched."

"Looks like you'd better tell Tony about this place." He turned around and pulled out his camera. Snapping the area of possible graves and some stray stones, he took nearly thirty photos. "Better get these leaves, too," he said and snapped the indentations up close. Taking one last shot of the broken limbs, he turned off the camera.

"You'll be careful, Edwin?" I said. "Rattlesnakes of the human kind are probably more dangerous to you."

He grinned and nodded. "Been here a long time. Ain't no human snake or haint goin' to scare me off."

I wasn't so sure, but Edwin appeared content as he checked on his reptilian zoo. We waved good-bye and headed back to the canoe.

"We'll see Tony in few hours," Harry said as he got into his van. "I'll take the camera."

I stood on the porch and waited for his taillights to fade into the trees. The forest was quiet, and there were no boats on the water. A broken twig sounded on the swamp floor and made me jump. I laughed, figuring it was Plato coming home for supper.

Back inside, I brushed leaves and brambles from my clothes and decided on a quick change before calling Pasquin. Our usual routine was for him to walk to my house and I'd take him wherever he needed to go. But I was uneasy about that. I didn't want him walking out there in almost darkness with some nut who followed people around.

Tossing the jeans and shirt in the hamper, I put on another outfit nearly the same. I pulled on the high boots again. The idea was to meet Pasquin halfway if I could.

No one answered his phone when I called, and the hair began to stand on my neck. Checking the clock, it was close to five-thirty. I hoped he had already left. Heading downstairs, I pulled on the jacket and patted the gun. Outside, I expected to be greeted by a hungry Plato, but no dog came panting to my feet.

I locked my door and left the screened porch. Heading toward the path that led into the swamp and eventually to Pasquin's house, I was afraid. The shadows were spreading this time of day, and in an hour it would be pitch black on the tree canopied lane. I moved slowly, using a small flashlight when I came upon a particularly dark spot. Once I stopped dead still, thinking I heard leaves move, only to see an armadillo pushing his way through some brush. I kicked his way, and he rolled into a silent ball that blended into the background colors.

By the time I had gone half way to Pasquin's house, I had heard a deer, a screech owl, and enough frogs to drown out any predatory human steps. Breathing a sigh of relief, I stood in front of the old man's house. A light was shining on the porch, a sure sign he had either left or was expecting a visitor.

"Pasquin!" I shouted when he didn't answer my knock. I nearly kicked myself when I realized I'd left his key back at the house.

He used to keep one on the outside, but I talked him out of that. "And now look where I am," I said to the elements. I walked around the outside. His windows were all heavily curtained. No one would be able to see anyone inside. In the back, I checked his work shed. Cluttered with a lifetime of rakes, hoes, shovels, wheel barrows, and containers of all kinds, it would not be an easy place for someone to hide, but it had been done before. I stood at the edge and said his name. There was no response.

I had moved to the other side of the house when I heard a rattle of glass and metal coming from the shed. Turning back and pulling the gun, I was in time to see two squirrels darting from the shed to the trees. Movement from the back of the place told me what I needed to know. Pasquin had a squirrel problem in that shed and if anything back there could be gnawed on, they were doing it.

Walking to his landing, I finally breathed a sigh of relief. Pasquin's boat was not there. I turned and nearly ran the distance back to my house.

"You old goat!" I said as I approached the porch. "I thought you had been kidnapped."

"Took the boat," he said. "It's getting a bit too cold to walk down that path late at night."

"Listen, Edwin thought he heard someone following us today."

"Yep. He told me. Only he said spying on you."

"When did you talk to him?" I marveled at the ways of swamp people and how word traveled fast.

"He took his boat out just after you left. Brought me a new hat band." He held up a snake skin that had been treated and sewed to fit around the old straw hat Pasquin used as more of a security blanket than a sun block.

CHAPTER TEN

Reverend Jensen had chosen a spot on the other side of his church for his Halloween feast. The little white church itself sat like a punctuation mark between two sides of history—the ancient primitive rites of the dead and the crime scene tape of a modern forensics lab. Both celebrated the dead, if celebrate was the word.

Pasquin came to the party with me, dragging along his straw hat and wearing an army surplus coat.

"Why don't you buy a wool beret or some warmer hat for this weather?" I asked as I edged the Honda into a small space within a long line of vehicles at the side of the road. We were going to have to walk nearly half a mile.

"Beret don't fan good," he said and shoved the straw one on top of his white hair.

People poured out of trucks, vans, cars, even off a couple of motorcycles. Most had young costumed children with them. Excitement spread among Supermen, Cinderellas, and Draculas. Even the clowns and fairies darted about dangerously in front of cars. The adults carried grocery bags most likely filled with candy to distribute once the fish eating was done. Near the front of the car line, two large trucks unloaded cooking supplies.

In the clearing, the men of the church had dug their fire pits and placed the cauldrons on the stands. A row of portable tables made a large box shape around three sides of the area. There was just enough room between the tables and the trees for women to stand and put together the cornmeal, egg, onion, and spice for the hush puppies. They mixed the ingredients then rolled them into the size of golf balls and stacked them in a wide metal pan with high sides.

The men had poured grease into one cauldron and waited for it to heat. Once it did, they tossed in the hush puppies and let them brown, then ladled them out and onto platters lined with paper towels.

In another cauldron, the men heated water. They turned this one over to some women who dumped in bags of grits and stirred them until time to add cheddar cheese. The stirring would continue until the grits and cheese mixed into a soft, yellow consistency. These would be ladled directly onto individual plates alongside the fish.

The third cauldron stood away from the others. It was heating grease, too, and men stood behind a nearby table, hacking at fish caught in the past few days, scaling, gutting and pushing all the parts that wouldn't be eaten into large plastic cans. The edible parts were passed to a group of women who coated them in egg and corn meal and placed them where the cooks could drop them into the oil. Frying took only minutes, and helpers stood by with large pans, filling them and taking them to the food table. No one bothered with tongs. People just picked up pieces of fried fish and placed them next to the hush puppies and grits.

The last place on the tables held the many plastic containers of homemade cole slaw. Church women had volunteered to make it, and the taste varied with which container you chose. Some used dill, some added sugar, others added raisins and pineapple bits—a favorite with the kids— but the best ones to me added grated sweet onions into the shredded cabbage.

"Oh, this place smells like heaven!" said Pasquin as we pushed our way between two wizards to the food tables.

Just before the entrance, Jensen had placed a well-made box with a slit and a lock. It was fastened atop a wooden pedestal with a sign that read DONATIONS. I shoved in ten dollars. Others put in bills and the children were raised up by their parents to drop in quarters.

"He's got this well organized," I said.

"Nothing like a church group to put together something like this," said Pasquin. "Only thing missing is the beer, or whiskey jug." He laughed. "And a little dancin' music."

"Plenty of pagan demons running around." I watched a row of witches compare each other's costumes and begin to fly about on toy brooms.

"Guess it's okay if the church sanctions it."

"More like okay if the church profits from it," I said.

"Your friends are in the crowds," said Pasquin.

Standing near the grove of trees and not yet moving toward the donation box, Tony and Marshall Long viewed the situation. Marshall came for the food and I glimpsed him staring at the cooking cauldrons more than once. He wore a huge flannel shirt that wasn't tucked into his oversized jeans. Tony's dress was the same, only his shirt was tucked into neatly pressed jeans.

A hand touched my elbow.

"Keep your eye on Jensen, okay?" Vernon squeezed my arm. "We got word that Reverend Billy is going to show up, and that could provide a bit of tension."

"There's someone Billy is going to have even more tension with," I said and nodded toward the statuesque Olivia Jourdain. She stood tall and proud, but only too obviously worried about venturing onto the scene. She was too well dressed in black slacks with a matching jacket and an orange sweater.

"This is my niece, Danielle, whom we call Dandy," she said as she approached me. "She decided this might be more fun than going door to door." She smiled at a little girl who came up to her knees and was dressed in an African tunic. Her little head seemed over-burdened with a colorful turban that matched the dress.

"Beautiful costume," I said and shook the girl's hand. She smiled and moved behind her aunt.

"She's a bit shy," said Olivia. She turned toward her niece and looked back at the entrance just in time to see Preacher Billy arrive with two women. "Oh, lord, here we go," she said.

"And the Folsom family is across the road," I said when I spied the old man, his son, and grandson standing on the other side behind some cars. They didn't seem to be trying to hide, but they clearly were not going to join the party.

Olivia allowed her eyes to stray from Billy to the Folsom's. "This isn't going to get really nasty, is it?" She hugged her niece closer to her legs.

"There's also a great deal of law enforcement here, Ms. Jourdain. I don't think they're going to let things get crazy."

She let her eyes move over the crowd. "Not in uniform?"

I nodded and pointed her towards the donation box and away from Billy, who had by now realized there was a very tall woman standing in his path. He stopped dead still and glared at her back as she moved away.

"We brought two children," he said to me almost because I was the only one standing there. "Where do they go?"

I shrugged. "They can join the rest of the goblins who are running about or stay with you. Reverend Jensen hasn't said anything yet."

As though on cue, someone dragged a kitchen ladder to the

edge of the donation box and Jensen climbed to the top. His blond presence towered above the crowd, and he used his strong voice to yell for quiet. Parents shushed their kids and stopped them in their tracks.

"Welcome all!" Reverend Jensen held up both arms as though gathering his flock. "This is our first Halloween fish fry, and I hope all of you make the most of it." He lowered his arms and cleared his voice. "Just a few rules, and please all the little imps out there listen to this." He laughed at himself. "No walking or running in the cemetary or sitting on the graves, no matter how tempting that may be. We must respect the living families. Also, beyond the cemetery, the sheriff has yellow tape cordoning off their scene. It's also on the Folsom property and we are not to interfere with it in any way. Now, after we have our fill of the fish supper, we'll give out Halloween candy near my trailer, next to the expertly carved pumpkin." He pointed and laughed again. "And I might remind you to use the trash bins set up at the edge of the road."

"Let's all bow our heads," he said, suddenly breaking the festive mood. Again with both hands in the air, he said the prayer of thanks. Some of the church people put their hands in the air, too, as did Bill and the two women who stood at his side.

"You don't put your arms up, you won't receive the grace," Pasquin whispered behind me.

"Somehow, I feel like the witches crossing the moon are going to deflect these prayers," I whispered back.

"Evil woman, you!" He chuckled low, the only sound I heard outside of Jensen's booming prayer.

As soon as people opened their eyes, they headed for the food tables. The first area held the paper plates and plastic silverware. Beyond that, a woman arranged paper cups for soda or iced tea.

She poured either sweet or unsweet tea into cups and a helper reached into the cooler beneath the table to drag out diet or regular cans of soda. Like locusts in Job, the crowd moved in an organized manner from plates, to drinks, to slaw, then hush puppies, and fish. Many had brought lawn chairs and made circles on the church grounds, or sat on the steps. The kids used the grass, some coming within inches of the grave stones.

While the kids ate, three grown-ups began setting up the entertainment. One woman donned a headscarf tied at the back and attached hoop earrings to her earlobes and a red fringed gown over her clothes. She placed a blue decorative garden globe on a portable table and two stools on either side. Sitting beneath a tree, she was in near darkness. Her globe table had a small shelf where she placed a hurricane lamp, the old-fashioned kind that used a candle behind thick glass. The flickering light jumped off the tree shadows and put her face in an eerie light. She would read palms or the aura of some kid who wanted a fortune told. Cards were just too evil for this church.

A few steps away, a young man erected a fold-out puppet theatre and set up hand puppets, witches, ghosts, and something that looked like a cowboy hero. He spread a large cloth on the ground close to the theatre, where the kids would sit until the routine pushed them to more active spooks.

The last section was an old man who sat on a chair he had pulled from the back of his truck. He built a small fire in front and waited for children to sit in a circle. His large floppy black hat cast a shadow over his eyes. To finish off the sinister look, he wrapped a black cape around his shoulders. He was the ghost story teller.

All three of these people ate from full plates as they awaited their audiences.

I leaned against a tree near the entrance. Tony and Vernon joined me.

"You found another grave site," said Tony. "Any sign of bones?"

"None," I said. "Harry checked it out. He says it could be an old site but the etching in the stone was done recently. And the shells were put there recently. Could be somebody is trying to keep up the place, or fake it. You might want to check it out."

"Way back in the woods behind Edwin's house," said Pasquin who joined us with two plates piled with fish fixings. He handed one to me.

"Is there no legend or record of any kind?" Tony picked at one piece of fish on his plate.

"Harry's going to look into it," I said.

"Never heard of it myself," Pasquin said. "But you got to know this old swamp is full of legends about graves. I bet if you talked to every old swamp rat around, you'd get just as many stories."

"Did I hear you say there was another slave grave site?" The soft voice of Olivia Jourdain came from the side. Even with her height, she was able to hide her presence in the shadows.

"We aren't sure," I said when the men seemed dumbfounded. "It's a clearing and the anthropologists will check it out."

"I need to be in on that," she said. "I expect to be called if any soil turning is done. Even if you use ground sonar, I want to be there."

Tony shifted on his feet, his jaw tightening in agitation. "Not in the beginning, ma'am. We'll let you know when you can come."

"Is it a crime scene, then?" She asked and stiffened.

"Not yet, but we need to find out first."

"I don't think so," she said and turned away. We watched her walk into the shadows again.

"Now all we need is to get Preacher Billy started," said Pasquin.

Marshall Long had returned to the food table and headed our way with a feast on his plate.

"Best Halloween party I've been to this year," he said, lifting a fried fish filet in the air and eating it like a carrot stick. "Only thing lacking is tartar sauce."

"That's not Southern," said Vernon.

"Is now." Marshall tossed a whole hush puppy into his mouth.

In the distance, Preacher Billy laughed and chatted with some old men, men who in the past would not have allowed him near the premises. Even the elegant Olivia would not have been welcome forty years ago. I smiled at how things like this had changed for the better.

The two women who came with Billy, dressed in pants suits they would have worn to church, stayed together but made friendly conversation with Jensen's crowd. They kept a close watch on the two children who played with the others. In between bites of food, they chased each other and tried to act scary. It all ended with laughter and food on the ground.

Olivia said something to her niece who had found a similarly shy girl dressed as an angel and was sitting on a napkin spread on the grass. The girl nodded, and Olivia walked away from her, towards Billy.

Even from across the relative darkness of the area, I could see Billy stiffen at her approach. He wiped his hand on the napkin he had tucked into his shirt and shook her hand. The two stood and chatted.

"Animated but not angry," I said when I nudged Vernon to look at them. "Think they'll get into it here?"

Before he could answer, Billy's face went serious and he looked sharply in my direction.

"She's told him something," said Vernon, "and I'll bet it's about the site you found."

"Oh, joy," said Tony. "We'll have to get somebody out there to guard the place."

"Don't see why," said Pasquin. "All we got to do is tell Edwin not to be a guide. He won't. Plus, they'll take one look at his backyard and run the other way."

"Maybe others know the swamp like he does," said Tony.

"You got one of them cell phones? I can give him a call right now."

Tony nodded. I pulled out my cell and punched the number for him. Pasquin started to yell into the phone but I put my finger to my mouth just in time. He gave the message to Edwin.

"He says okay. He'll keep it all a secret. But, he won't guarantee somebody won't find their own way out there."

People still kept coming to the party, even some who had been trick-or-treating in spite of the dangers. Harry strolled in late and refused to eat the fish.

"I've seen too much of the lake waters where they caught the things," he said and laughed. "Besides, I had steak."

Not long after he arrived, Carl, Dalton, and Lily came in giggling and stumbling over each other. They had tote bags with long straps slung over their shoulders.

"Is the fish good?" Lily burst into laughter and nearly dropped her bag. "Oops! Mustn't lose a drop." She pulled a bottle in a paper bag out of her tote and took a swig.

"This is a church!" Pasquin said as the rest of us stared in amazement.

"We just dropped by," said Carl who was equally into giggles. Only Dalton stared wide-eyed at the crowd.

"Are they on the graves?" he asked.

"Been warned not to be," said Pasquin, the only one of us

who felt like talking to the overgrown teens.

"Isn't there a football game or something, you could go to tonight?" Tony frowned at them, knowing he may have to do something about the beer they had in their bags.

"School night, man!" Carl laughed and threw back the last swig from his bottle. He walked to one of the bins and tossed it away with the soda cans.

"I'm going to eat," said Dalton and shoved his glasses farther up his face. He walked stiffly away from the others and grabbed a plate for food.

"Well," said Lily, shaking her head in a mocking manner. "What's he pissed about?"

"Maybe he's pissed because both of you are royally pissed," I said.

They stood quiet for a moment then burst out laughing. Before they said anything else, we moved away from them. They sat down on the ground in the shadow of a tree and opened new bottles.

"Baptists won't like that," I said.

"Nor any of the other denominations out here tonight." Vernon took my hand and led me to the edge of Jensen's trailer.

The story teller, a man older than Pasquin had pushed a plastic skull into the center of a semicircle of kids, just at the edge of his fire, and was kidding them about ghosts. He began to talk in the sing-song way of the old people and told them the story of the spirits you could see coming up from a slimy pond on a winter's night.

"It's not good to let a pond get slimy," he said in a low whisper. "Gets uncomfortable for the drowned bodies down there."

He stood up slowly, his old knees cracking. As he rose, he lifted his hands in the air and spoke in a shaky voice. "And they rise up like mist off the water, only they're greenish, and they say hello to the vultures in the trees. Them birds just stare down from the dark cypress, waiting for something to die." The old man stopped and waited for the kids to giggle. None did. "But them spirits move through the trees and find them an old house where there are cracks in the wall or a window is open, and they just float right inside. All the people are asleep, and that ghosty fog passes over each one, taking his soul for the water." He eased back down on the stool.

Looking directly at the kids, he asked, "Ever see mist floating amongst the trees at night?" He stayed silent until a couple nodded their heads. "Well, that's the slimy pond spirits. And, you know what?" He waited just long enough for them to give full attention. "Sometimes them spirits bring one of them vulture birds right inside with them. 'Specially if the window is open. Spirit moves in so silent you don't know it, but when it gives the signal, WHOOSH! in flies the black vulture." He slapped his hands together when he blew in the bird. Everyone jumped, including the adults on the edge of the circle. The kids screamed and broke into rolling laughter on the ground.

"They laugh now," I said, "but I wonder how many will close the windows and watch for fog in the woods tonight."

I watched the old story teller take out a handkerchief and wipe his mouth. Behind him and a few yards away, Olivia walked slowly with Reverend Jensen, the two in deep conversation. He took her elbow, and they moved into the shadows behind his trailer.

CHAPTER ELEVEN

The men and women at the food tables began to clear up just before midnight. Jensen had promised the kids he'd hold the candy part until near the witching hour, and he was now ready. He had lit a candle in the crudely carved pumpkin on his doorstep and nodded for the volunteers to start handing out the candy.

Many of the adults drifted to their cars. Engines started in the darkness. The fires in the pits were put out by the men who tended the cauldrons. As the kids lined up with their treat bags, some almost nodded off where they stood. Smiling when the candy hit the bottom of the bag, they turned and joined their parents who would have to wake them in the car before tucking them into bed.

Lily and Carl dozed against the side of the church. Dalton paced in front of them.

"Can you drive, son?" asked Tony.

"Of course," he said, his eyes wide with fear.

"Then we'll help you get these two into the car." He motioned for Vernon, Harry, and a uniform deputy to follow him.

The four of them grabbed hold of Lily and Carl, who woke up suddenly and laughed at their predicament.

"We're being toted to jail!" said Carl.

"Off to the gallows!" giggled Lily.

"The best place for a hanging," said Carl.

"Shut up!" Dalton yelled at both.

"Okay, nice boy," said Carl. "We'll hush." He placed his finger to his mouth. Lily did the same. Both suppressed laughter.

When the three college students had shoved themselves into the van that belonged to Carl who had handed over the keys, Dalton did his best to get onto the road and take off in a mad hurry.

"Hope that boy don't hit somebody down the road," said Pasquin.

We stood just outside the church grounds, facing the dark road that led to the main highway. Other cars turned on their lights as they traveled home with weary kids and even wearier parents.

Behind us, we could hear Preacher Billy speaking in a loud voice.

"Why don't you come visit our church some Sunday? You might get a whiff of real history in action. We still do it like the old folks did." He laughed, and the echo resounded through the trees.

"I don't need to do that, sir," said Olivia, her voice nearly trembling with anger. "I believe in keeping the past alive but not to the extent of being a slave."

"I didn't say that!" Billy nearly yelled.

"It's just a figure of speech." Olivia's voice spat out in a vicious whisper. "I meant I don't have to live like people did in history to appreciate what they did to get us where we are today."

"And," said one of the women who stood by Billy, "where are we today? Playing with white society?"

"Playing?" Olivia turned away, then turned back again to face the three people. "I am not playing anything. I have a good position and I got there by my own merits." She bent close to the woman's face. "Don't you ever accuse me of playing white! Not ever!" She reached up and swatted the woman's hat hard enough to knock it into the dusty road.

"Now, now," said Billy, taking on the demeanor of diplomat. "We respect your position. We just keep some of the old ways."

"Keep them, then! Just stay out of my way when I fight to keep the respect for our burial grounds." Olivia turned away, grabbed her niece by the hand, and marched to her car.

Pasquin and I stayed silent for a long time.

Tony and Vernon appeared on the road, and Billy went into his greeting routine. He must have repeated it every Sunday at the church door.

"Detective Amado!" He bowed slightly and shook Tony's hand. He turned to Vernon and did the same to him. "You must come hear a sermon at our church at least once in your life." He laughed. So did I. The thought of the stiff Tony in an emotional church like that was comic.

"Just do us a favor," said Tony, ignoring the invitation. "Keep everyone out of these cemeteries. There's something more than history going on, and I don't want anyone to get hurt."

"Not to mention accused of anything," said Billy. His laugh this time tried too hard, the phoniness made clear.

Billy and the two women and the children piled into their large black car and left, fading quickly into the shadows.

"Let's go inspect the scene. See if anyone did any damage," said Tony, keeping his eyes on the road.

We turned to enter the church grounds again. The donation box was gone, most likely locked inside the church or maybe in Jensen's rattle trap of a trailer. A few couples were still cleaning up, women wiping the tables until the men folded them and placed them in a storage room in back of the church. The cauldrons had been covered but they would have to wait for morning to be cleaned.

"Nice gathering!" said Jensen as we approached his trailer. He was snuffing the candle inside the pumpkin.

"You had a few guests I imagine you didn't expect," said Tony.

"You mean Preacher Billy? He's okay. He probably came to see that no one ran over the grave site."

"The Folsom's were across the road," I said.

"Oh, they wouldn't walk on these grounds for an event. They'd like it if we just pulled up and moved. Won't happen." Jensen shook his head as he gathered the large pumpkin in his arms and headed for the trash bins. "They came to make sure no one trespassed on their land."

"I never saw any 'No Trespassing' signs," I said.

"Not any, but they still don't want people stomping around out there." He turned and laughed. "Might step in a volcano hole." He bellowed this out and nodded his head toward the tree line where the Folsom three stood like warlocks guarding the portal to hell.

"Look what I got one of the ladies to make up for me," said Marshall. He carried two paper plates full of food and covered in plastic wrap. "Won't have to cook for a week."

"You cook?" said Pasquin. "That won't last you till morning."

"Never mind, Marshall," said Tony, shooting a frown toward the Folsom's, "you'll find plenty to eat somewhere. Now what about the bones. Anything else?"

"Come around tomorrow afternoon. We may have all the pieces together as far as we can tell. Lots missing. You might have those dredgers go through some of the mud in and around the pond."

Tony nodded and watched as Marshall balanced his plates until he got to his van where he placed them gently on top. He opened the rear and, amongst boxes of gloves, collection receptacles, and forensic test packages, he set them so they wouldn't spill.

"Think that boy can tell fish bone from knuckles?" Pasquin laughed at himself.

I said my goodnights to Vernon, wishing I could join him at his lake house again. But, he was on duty after a day off, and I had to take Pasquin to his boat.

We arrived with only the headlights giving us vision of anything.

"Are you sure you can manage that thing on the water at this hour?" I followed Pasquin to the landing where he had tied up his motor boat.

"Been doing it nearly eighty years, ma'am," he said and bent over with a grunt to untie the rope. "Don't plan on having trouble now."

I knew it was no use to argue. I watched him start the boat, tip his hat to me, and disappear around a bend of trees. His sole boat light lasted until it, too, faded in the darkness.

Hearing a flap, I looked up into the cypress trees. The black birds had gathered there again, sitting like they had been invited to haunt the land on Halloween night. Their erect stillness sent chills down my spine.

"Hope one doesn't come 'whooshing' into my window tonight," I said as I headed inside and to bed.

Dawn brought dog and a cold mist off the river. Plato scratched at the door and barked a few times before I could manage to get downstairs. I shivered. It would soon be time to turn on the heat.

"Mutt! It's not even six in the morning. Where have you been?"

I sometimes wondered just what he'd answer if he could. He found something or someone of interest out there, taking up with who knows what, and returning when he needed a store bought meal.

I opened the dog food and scooped it into his bowl while he lapped water. Without even a tail wag, he went from water dish to food and gulped as though he lived in the wild and another animal would get his meal if he didn't finish it quickly.

"I guess you have been in the wild," I said and stroked his side. His fur was cold and a bit damp from the fog.

As soon as I had showered, the phone rang.

"Tony has called a meeting of all involved. Can you meet this afternoon at Marshall Long's lab office?" Vernon sounded tired. He had been called out twice for disturbances at the bar where Nuggin Ires had done his dirty business.

"Nuggin, by the way, showed up across the river," he added. "Somebody gave him a ride and he passed out in a bar down near the bridge. Slept it off in the old boat house outside the bar."

The cold caught the students by surprise once again. Many wanted to dress in summer stock, but they had to drag out jackets to pull over their shorts. Bare legs broke into goose bumps before they made it across campus to their first class.

"Manny, do you own heavier shoes?" I said as he walked into his office with the old sandals around bare feet.

"Nope. I might put on some wool socks, but I like these. Don't make fun of my shoes." He placed some papers on his desk. "Senior projects," he said. "Who said it was the department chair's duty to approve them?"

"You, as I recall," I smiled. Paperwork was the bane of all teachers, eventually giving the final shove into retirement.

"All I do is take the faculty advisor's word that it's an okay subject." He tapped a pencil on top of the stack.

"Including the one about morgue lingo?"

"Why not?" he shrugged. "You can find vocabulary anywhere on the subject, but maybe he'll come up with a new pattern. And, with the advent of new forensics, there could be stuff not in the literature—linguistic literature, I mean."

"You've just given your approval for Carl Mabry to begin."

"Guess so. He says he's got contacts."

I didn't wait for any more of Manny's justifications for the projects. He'd approve all of them, and many would go on to graduate school and expand them into their thesis work.

Inside the building where I taught my first class, I watched the crowded halls empty as students hurried into warmer spots. Just as I went into my own room, I saw a wheelchair come down the middle with Dalton pushing it.

"Look who's out of the hospital and back to school," he said. He kept his eyes down.

"Reena!" I looked down at the girl, her sullen face not at all happy about the situation. "How are you feeling?"

She looked up at me, an angry flash coming from her eyes. "I'm not feeling anything," she said. "They gave me pain pills, but I don't even feel that, just some tingling off and on."

"The doctor says that's good. It will get better." Dalton's awkwardness was even more pronounced as he tried to comfort her.

"I guess these turkeys are going to have to push me around for a while," she gestured toward her back where Dalton looked more astonished than amused.

"They won't mind," I said, and tried to smile.

"Serves them right!" She motioned for Dalton to move and they continued down the hallway.

The day dragged on with my lectures and demonstrations of topics I had covered for years. There had been some new stuff come out, but even that after a few semesters feels like old hat. The student questions were the same year after year, and I had to remind myself that the students themselves were different each year. The questions were new to them.

By the time I drove to Marshall's office, I was asking myself if forensic scientists had the same old questions. The field seemed to be booming with new things to find out "who done it."

When I met with the others in the bone room off his office, I realized that his field had to rely on an older foundation of information just as mine did.

"We got most of the bones put together right, we think, and we determined the bones found in this county are from the same bodies as those found on the Folsom land," he said as he stood behind three metal tables. Each table held enough bones to make out human skeletons without heads. "Pretty easy to match the cut patterns."

"Skull caps," he said and pointed to the rounded bones at the top of two skeletons. "If we had the entire skull, me might have teeth for DNA. As it is, we're working on getting it from a few other bones. But," he drew this out in a long breath, "we've been able to match the sawed ends of the body bones."

"Any idea who sawed them?" asked Tony.

"Funny you should ask that." Marshall picked up one of the bones from an arm. "Nice work, right?" He ran his hand along the obvious cut joint. "And look at the skull cap." He held that up, turning it to make the edge visible. "Fine job."

"You're saying it was a specialized saw?" said Tony.

"Specialized in that it was a surgical saw," he said. "Like this one." He held up the instrument used to cut through a sternum or cranial bone in an autopsy procedure. When Marshall turned it on, its small round blade whirred in the air. "I can't be positive because I don't know carpenter's saws all that well, but I think this is what he used to cut these people apart."

"Embalmed people, old people, surgical saw," I said. "Are we dealing with a funeral home, a pathologist, or just someone who knows how to use one of these things?"

"Not my job," said Marshall, "but how many just plain lay people out there have a saw like this?"

Marshall hooked his finger and led us back to his office. He grabbed a bag from his desk and waved it about the room.

"Remember this? It's the plastic cup and hamburger wrapper Luanne pulled from the pond in the dive. The wrapper was crumpled enough and greasy enough to hold a partial finger print in spite of the water. Now, all we have to do is find someone to match it with. It's not in the data base." He dropped the bag to the desk. "Of course, it could be anyone who smooches in that area. May not have anything to do with sawed bones."

Tony's cell phone rang.

"It's Loman. He's late but he's got some data for us. He'll be here in twenty minutes." He turned to Marshall. "You got a place we can meet in anywhere around here?"

We sat in a long narrow room at a long narrow table. Marshall himself insisted on the end seat because his girth made it uncomfortable to wedge into a side chair. Loman was still breathing hard when he reached the room. He placed three folders on the table.

"You got the floor," said Tony who knew the sergeant would wait for his cue.

"Well, I've been doing the search on funeral homes like you said. Nobody is reporting bodies missing. Almost all of them are skittish because of that place up in Alabama that got into all the trouble a couple of years back. They make sure the coffin goes to the site and is lowered there." He flipped open the top file. "Two places have reported vandalism at new graves. Mostly spray painting on the tombstones or sticking devil symbols on the top of the grave. Nothing that looks like bodies have been dug up."

"Could it have happened prior to burial?" I asked.

"Don't see how," Loman said. "Like the directors said, they're keeping a close eye on things. They don't like law suits."

"Then these bodies could be from somewhere else?" asked Vernon.

"Could be. Maybe when the lab does DNA we'll know."

Marshall shook his head. "Even if we get it, if there is no match in some other data base, we won't be able to identify anyone. And let me add, these bones are from elderly people. Most people that age have no reason to have their DNA in a data bank."

Loman sighed, his sleepy eyes adding sadness to the futility of the task.

"What's in the other folders?" asked Tony.

"These aren't finished, but I've got people doing background checks on anyone around that site, anyone who went on the tours."

I looked around the room. "Shouldn't Detective Folsom be here?"

"We'll fill him in later," said Tony. It was a quick answer, one with a bit of guilt. "Go on, Loman."

"The most interesting so far is the Reverend Jensen. He got into a bunch of trouble in his last church. Now, he told Luanne about some of it if you remember. But, he mostly mentioned being accused of taking money. That's never been proved. The women he got involved with have been proved."

"Women?" We asked in unison.

"Yeah, women, single mothers of young kids."

CHAPTER TWELVE

"He showed no signs of trying to touch the kids at the fish fry," I said. "I don't trust him, but I don't trust anyone who stands at a pulpit and tells me how to get into heaven."

"You said he confessed to you about the money mix-up?" Tony took a walk around the table as though pacing would help his thought processes. It just made the rest of us nervous.

"Yes. In the car when we went to visit Reena at the hospital. He said he wanted to clear that up, because he knew you'd find out."

"But nothing about women?" He stared at me. "Or kids?"

"Tony, if you're asking if he made advances toward me in any way on that trip into town and back, the answer is no. He made me uneasy because he's a 'holy man' and I don't know how to act around them. I'm always afraid they're going to start in on the proselytizing and I'll have to chop them down."

"Could be the women were agreeable," Tony shrugged. "What does the record say?"

"Two women at different times. The first one left her husband for him. Didn't move in as he was living in the manse, but took a place near by. Her husband filed for divorce on grounds of adultery and went after custody of the kids. He made accusations against Jensen, but they weren't proved. Kids said nothing happened."

"That's pretty standard divorce fare," said Vernon. "If you can prove something with the kids, it goes against that party."

"It didn't last, evidently." Loman picked up the paper and read a paragraph. "All charges were dropped. She returned to her husband, and Jensen was warned by the congregation. Put on probation, in fact."

"Are you saying probation wasn't enough to keep his pants zipped?" I asked. Tony stared at me, his jaw tightened. Vernon smiled and looked at the floor.

"Couple of years later, he got involved with another woman with young kids, boy and a girl, just like before. This time, the husband didn't care. He took off for parts unknown and the woman had to support all three of them. Jensen got her an apartment not too far from the manse. Maybe he thought this was okay since her husband flew the coup."

"But it wasn't?"

"These are Baptists, aren't they?" Loman's sleepy eyes lit up with his own humor. "Man and woman aren't married. Two kids involved, and he's been accused of liking kids more than their mumsy."

"Don't tell me, they asked him to leave?" Marshall spoke to the ceiling.

"Yep. Fired him. Again with nothing proved, he was able to get another church—this one."

Marshall laughed. "Down in the Southern piney woods where incest is as common as mosquitoes and nobody asks questions if the church lady takes a pan of fried chicken and apple dumplings to the poor minister with no wife."

We all looked at each other. Tony wouldn't sit down.

"Anybody been inside that trailer of his?"

Heads shook around the table.

"Well, we need to find a way to get in there." Tony sighed as though he had found a solution. "Offhand, I can't think of a reason to get a search warrant."

When no one responded, Tony changed the subject to the cemetery search. Loman pulled up another folder and gave sketchy news.

"Not much. That case in Alabama got all these guys on their toes. Ain't nobody going to dump bodies in the woods all the while pretending they buried them."

"Any complaints at all?"

"One couple over in Sneads said they heard rumors of people digging in the cemetery late at night and insisted on their grannie being dug up for assurance."

"And, were they assured?" Tony asked, his eyes glaring at Loman to hurry the pace.

"It was grannie all right. The couple decided to remove her two rings just in case somebody did start digging and robbing corpses." He smiled.

"Yeah," said Vernon, "like the couple themselves. I'll bet they did that to get those rings when they realized they weren't in grannie's old house."

"Pretty much what the sheriff thinks over there, too, but the funeral home wouldn't go further with it. They were just glad nothing was amiss."

"More?" Tony paced, his hands on his hips.

"Only a couple of cases where the funeral home got the body in the wrong place. Mixed up the plots people had bought. They straightened it out and moved the bodies." Loman closed the file. "That's it."

Tony finally sat down. He was deep in thought, his jaw working in agitation.

"What's in the third folder?" asked Marshall.

Tony jumped and stared at Loman. He frowned. I wanted to laugh. He hated when he slipped up like that, even if it was just overlooking a folder.

"I played around a bit with the other players in this scene," said Loman. "Time drags waiting for reports to come in." He picked up the folder and opened it.

"Now, here's your history lady, Miss Olivia Jourdain. Only she really hasn't been a 'Miss' all that long. Married three times to white men, once to a black man. None lasted more than a year."

We all stared at him. Olivia Jourdain, the classy intellectual who let Preacher Billy embarrass her had jumped marriage four times.

"Did you check on the husbands?" I asked.

"All four, either business men or in the case of the final one, a professor. He's still here. A visiting academic from Kenya, he calls himself."

"Don't tell me," I said, "anthropology?"

Loman smiled. "You read my mind."

"But no criminal record that you can find?" added Tony.

"None. Domestic disturbance with the second husband. Spousal abuse charged. Only it wasn't him on her; it was her on him. Guy was old and she took to hitting him. His grown children didn't like that." He flipped the page. "Nothing else."

"How did she make out in the divorces," I asked.

"Pretty good, except the professor from Africa. Got herself a tidy settlement and a nice house on the north side of town."

I nodded. Miss Jourdain never appeared to be a fool, but now I knew she was a foxy manipulator. Her frustration with Preacher Billy may not have been his social interaction, but the fact she couldn't get to him, seduce him in a way.

"And which husband was the Jourdain," I asked again.

"None. That's her maiden name. She never took on the married names."

"You have anything else in there?"

"Nothing finished. I'm still working on the college kids, and the old couples on the tour were about as bland as you get."

"Then we can leave?" Tony turned toward the door.

"Wait!" said Loman. "This is what I've got on the Folsom family for now." He held up several sheets of paper. "And they are a screwed up bunch."

"Tell us all about Southern incest," said Marshall, laughing at his own joke.

"Not too far off the track," said Loman. "That son, the middle one, was accused by his own sister of poking around where he shouldn't when they were teens. Made his daddy pretty mad and he sent him off to military school."

"Military school, or the place for bad boys?" asked Tony.

"Most likely the second chance boys' farm near the Georgia border," said Vernon. "I don't see any military remnants in Arnold, Jr."

"Detective Folsom also had his bad boy days. Got picked up a few times for drinking and racing cars. Nothing to stay in his record. Guess he got religion in his twenties and became a deputy."

"Yeah," said Marshall, "redeemed himself."

"You said you weren't finished?" I asked.

"This is just a superficial run on backgrounds. Folsom family is the kind you need to ask the surrounding neighbors about. Got skeletons all over the house, I'm sure."

Tony half smiled, then checked himself. "Okay, unless I need you for something, why don't you put on your overalls and go talk to some yokels?"

Loman smiled, his sleepy eyes dancing in agreement.

We left the building that housed body parts and pieces of evidence small enough to be seen only with a microscope, yet powerful enough to send men to the death chamber. In the parking lot, we huddled against a cold wind that had blown into the region. We waited for Tony to give orders, but he seemed irritated by the whole thing and unsure what to do next.

"Maybe we could go to church on Sunday," said Vernon, his wide grin teasing all of us.

"Don't knock it," said Tony. "It might tell us something."

It had to be a divine sign. As soon as everyone got quiet again, my cell phone rang. It was Pasquin.

"You got to get those deputies out here, Luanne. Edwin is in a dither all over my front room. He just doesn't know what to do."

"A dither about what?"

"He found something at that grave site he took you to the other day. A dead man." I could hear his voice fade as though turning his head toward Edwin. "A dead black man. His head bashed in."

"Can you take Edwin back to his place?" I said. "I'll bring the deputies, and that's the best place to get to the site. Besides, Edwin would know how to get us there quicker than anyone else."

The others looked at me and waited for an explanation.

"Dead black man at the grave site behind Edwin's place," I said, and as soon as I did, cells came out and orders were given.

We piled into a sheriff's department motor boat and raced to the spot where the river met the woods and nearly hid Edwin's little landing. His boat was tied there. He and Pasquin stood a ways back, their faces looking from the trees like two scared rabbits. Both faces were paler than the moon, one with thick white hair blowing in the breeze, the other with stiff stand-up black hair that hadn't seen a shampoo bottle in a week.

"It's a big man," said Edwin as he held the side of the boat. "He's black and I think I might have seen him before, but I can't remember his name." I bet he had never talked so fast in his life.

I glanced at Vernon as I joined him on the landing. My brain was jumping with the possibility but I dared not say it out loud.

We trudged behind Edwin through brambles and heavy trees. The light was fading, and Marshall brought up the rear with Pasquin. A uniform deputy carried the scene kit for him.

We reached the clearing and Edwin wouldn't venture further. "It's just beyond that tall pine." He pointed to the entrance he had taken me through on our excursion. "Just lying there on some flat ground."

Tony waved for everyone to stay put and told Vernon to follow him with his light. Both held the flashlights toward the ground, looking for tracks or signs of blood. They moved inside the trees, and for a rare moment, the entire forest seemed to hold its breath.

"Follow the same path," called Tony. "He's here all right."

Marshall, the deputy, and I moved to the trees and looked inside, following the lights Vernon and Tony shined on the ground.

The mass seemed black all over, black shoes, pants, shirt, and skin. Only the skin was too shiny, sleek. If the light had been better, it would have shown red around the big wound at the side of the head.

"Preacher Billy," I whispered in the silence. "I just had a feeling that's who it would be."

Tony was on the phone for scene techs. Vernon and the other deputy began taping off the area at the edge of the clearing. I moved back with Pasquin and Edwin.

"You said Preacher Billy?" asked Edwin, his hands trembling now.

I nodded, thinking it peculiar he'd get so scared now and still be able to handle snakes like shoe laces.

"You knew?"

"Well, not really knew, but I had a feeling."

"A premonition like?" Edwin's eyes grew wider.

"Based on the case, yes, I guess so." I stared at him.

"It's the man's spirit," he said. "He was telling you it was him. And I think he was telling me he was here."

"What do you mean, boy?" Pasquin grumbled at his friend.

"I heard something in here." He jabbed a finger at his head. "A sound that needed help or something. It scared me, but it drew me to that spot." Edwin pointed to the edge of the woods which was fast becoming a crowded crime scene.

"You heard something? Like what?" said Pasquin. He took the man's arm.

"Just a feeling like a sound in my head," he said and pulled away from Pasquin.

We stared at the snake man of the swamp. He was genuinely frightened of something supernatural. Pasquin finally shook his head and looked at me.

"Let's get you back home," he said and motioned for Edwin to follow him.

Edwin stood still until Pasquin looked back at him.

"Can I stay at your place tonight?"

Pasquin's eyes sparkled for a moment, and he smiled. "Go get yourself cleaned up first."

"He won't take a favorite snake to sleep with, will he?" I asked.

"Never has so far. He's nothing but a boy pushing fifty, you know. You won't believe how many times he's come to my house to sleep the night. Says he wants company, but I see the goose bumps and the whites of his eyes. He gets scared, like a kid."

"Yet he has live rattlesnakes in the back yard!"

"His security guards, Luanne. You got Plato. He's got hiss and rattle." Pasquin pushed some brush aside for me to follow him to Edwin's house. "We'll wait for him and take his boat to my place. It's going to be a regular ship's harbor at that little landing in a moment."

I left word with Vernon that we'd be at Pasquin's. It took a while for Edwin to check on his zoo and take a shower. By the time we reached Pasquin's landing in his boat, both men were ready for a "bourbon by the fire" as Pasquin put it. I opted out and took off with one of his flashlights down the lane to my house.

"Gladly give you a boat ride home," said Edwin. I declined. The man seemed at peace in the safety of Pasquin's furniture-packed living room. Besides, I wanted to walk and think.

Darkness hovered now like a cold black shroud. I pointed the light in front of my feet and watched carefully for any night prowlers. But it was cold out, and not many animals dangerous to humans were on the hunt. Still, the hungry snake might see a field mouse and surprise me. I heard some birds in the tall cypress trees on the river and wondered why they were here.

When leaves crackled in the trees to my left, I stopped cold. Something walked there, and from the rhythms, it sounded human.

CHAPTER THIRTEEN

Noises in the swamp are common, but when they follow your steps, walk when you walk, stop when you stop, you know there is a thinking presence there. It may be predatory, but with a purpose other than the next meal. In a hair-raised panic I turned my flashlight into the trees.

Something like two dim bulbs reflected my light and then darted into the brush. There was effort to hide the noise. Someone was running from me. I took off after the sound, suddenly more angry than afraid.

I stumbled around low bushes growing between the pines and oaks, even darted close to the pointed ends of palmetto bushes. Stopping to get my bearings according to the sound of running feet, I heard nothing. My fear returned, because now he could be anywhere—behind a bush, in a tree, behind me. I turned quickly again and saw nothing in the beam of light.

In the distance, I heard barking. "Plato!" I yelled to the familiar sound coming from the direction of my house. If someone was about, I was letting him know a dog was headed my way. "Come on, boy!"

Plato shot through the brush, stopped and sniffed my feet, growled a bit, then sat down and looked up at me.

"Is he gone?" Plato's tail wagged.

"Must be." I shined the light into the woods in a full circle.

"Okay, boy, let's go home."

Plato walked beside me the entire way, crowding the path. When we came to my porch, I searched it thoroughly, and checked all the doors and windows once inside. Plato followed me, smelling of everything, but getting alarmed about nothing.

Both of us finally hunkered down in the living room. I felt jittery, my skin breaking out in goose bumps every time a screech owl shrieked on his way to a kill.

Before midnight, Pasquin called. The ringing phone gave me a start, and Plato stood up, his coarse hair bristling.

"Been talking to Edwin," said Pasquin. He was a night owl, himself, and sometimes didn't think about others who had to get up in the morning. "He's telling me about a bridge Folsom built on his property this side of the county line."

"Folsom has property in this county, too?"

"Lots of it, it seems. Edwin has been trekking about a hunting range."

"I didn't realize Edwin hunted anything but snakes."

"Don't, but he says there's holes on that land and he goes there." I could hear Edwin saying something to Pasquin in the background. "Says he wears an orange vest like the hunters."

"I would hope so. Why is he telling you about this bridge?"

"Says there's lots of creeks and ponds on that land, and Folsom built the bridge so hunters don't have to wade with the alligators." There was a long silence and a rustling sound like a palm over the phone.

"Pasquin?"

"Sorry. Edwin wants to take us to this bridge. He thinks it's interesting."

I hesitated, but Edwin had led us to the site where Preacher Billy had been found, and I wasn't going to write him off as the swamp idiot now.

"I've got classes in the morning. Will three o'clock give us enough time?"

Again, the phone was muffled, but I could hear male voices discussing the issue.

"He says yes if you can drive us to Becker Road. It's closer from there."

"Can you meet me here?"

"We'll be on your porch..." Pasquin stopped because Edwin was saying something more to him. "He says he's got extra orange vests and will bring some for us. Guess I'll have to take him home in the boat first, but we'll see you tomorrow."

Tromping about the woods during hunting season was not my idea of a safe afternoon hike, and Edwin was being cryptic about what we'd see there. Maybe he didn't know, just sensed something at issue. He was good at that, kind of like an animal. I looked down and patted Plato's head. "Sorry, old boy."

Before my first class the next day, Manny stopped me in the hallway. He wanted to know if I could set up a meeting with Marshall Long or someone from the scene tech lab to schedule student observations.

"You're doing Carl Mabry's work for him, aren't you?"

"Just getting him some contacts. He says he's already got a mortuary set up. He'd like a crime lab, too."

"Sounds like he doesn't quite know what he wants." I still had doubts about this research, but Manny wasn't going to fight it. He had long wearied of steering students into inventive, fascinating subjects that needed to be done. All he wanted was for them to learn how to deal with data gathering and write a decent report.

"I'll give you Marshall's office phone, but Carl is going to have to make the call himself." I pulled out my address book and copied the number on a scrap of paper.

"Have a nice day," Manny said and turned to walk down the hallway to his office, his worn leather sandals squeaking on the polished floor.

"A nice day?" I repeated out loud. "He's finally made it to the seventies."

Heading out to my classroom building, I ran into Reena again. She had learned to propel herself in her wheelchair though not with much precision.

"I'm getting the hang of it," she said as I offered to help. "Better let me do it and make my mistakes." She got the wheels across the threshold and into the hall. "Lord knows I've make enough of them lately."

"Mistakes?"

"Don't you call falling into a hole in the woods a mistake? Especially when it nearly breaks your spine?" She wasn't laughing.

"Where are your helpers today?"

"I gave up on them. Carl and Lily seem to have something going, and stupid Dalton has lab work, he says."

"Lab work?"

She looked up at me, her eyes both bitter and fearful. She shrugged without answering. Waving, she propelled herself to the elevators.

I spent an hour and a half on phonetics. My next class was in the same room, and since no one used it between classes, I said I'd meet with anyone needing help right there. The only person who came was Olivia Jourdain.

"I knew you had a break. I thought I'd catch you while I could." She wore a purple suit with a silky white blouse. In another world, she would fit the image of a congresswoman.

"I guess the sheriff has been asking you questions?"

"Yes," she sighed. "I had to go through every one of my marriages. It was bad enough when I lived through them." She made an attempt to laugh.

"The last one may cause me trouble," she said. "But I was honest. I married him to keep him in this country. He needed a green card. Simple as that."

"The marriage was a sham, then?" This wouldn't sit well with either the sheriff or the feds.

"No, no! It was an affair. I mean," she hesitated and looked away from me. "I mean we were dating, but I didn't love him. I liked him—a lot. But the marriage was doing him a favor."

"And you divorced?"

She gave a half smile and nodded. "I didn't come here to talk about my marital life. That could take days. I wanted to invite you to my office and show you some of the work we're doing."

"I have to be somewhere at three o'clock. Can we make it tomorrow?"

"I'd rather order lunch today and you can eat with me. It won't take long to give you a hint of what we know." She opened her eyes in surprise at her own words. "About slave burial artifacts, I mean!"

"After my next class?"

She agreed, and I spent the rest of my break wondering what she could show me.

The next class on romance language linguistic history stretched out slowly with students who had never studied a foreign language trying to understand inflected endings and their changes over time. I could recite them in my sleep but somehow had to keep it fascinating for the new crop.

After a few hurried chats with two male students, I rushed to the building where Olivia held court over reports written by historians and archeologists, and debated with local politicians and landowners about preservation. Her job couldn't be easy.

"I've had chicken with alfredo pasta sent in," she said, handing me a plate with an African motif at the edge. "It's really quite good. It's from Corrina's Kitchen." She dipped out the chicken and pasta into my plate. "Nice Caesar salad, too."

This woman lived better than I did. Corrina's Kitchen was a place that had three or four dollar signs in its price information. It tended to cater to state legislators and downtown lawyers.

"Classy," I said.

Olivia smiled. "I won't have it any other way." She picked up a fork and ate with the grace of a monarch.

"They're going to release Billy's body in a few days," I said. "Sorry to talk about that subject at lunch." I cut the tender chicken. "Will you attend his funeral?"

"Oh my, yes," she said softly. "It has to be that way. He'll be an historical preservation, himself, after that." She gave a small laugh and took another bite of chicken. "Will you go, too?"

"The sheriff will expect most of us to be there," I said. "He was murdered, you know."

"So it seems." She let her hand rest on the plate and stared into the air.

We finished the meal. She poured a little brandy into two small glasses and winked. "No one knows, but since we can't drink wine with our lunch, a little after will go a long way."

The rich, brown liquid burned a bit as it went down, and I was happy she didn't serve more.

"Now," she said, "let me show you the prep room." She stood, nodding for me to follow her into a room to the rear of her desk.

"This is where we keep on-going stuff, things that haven't yet made it into any museum anywhere. Some has to be authenticated, and other things are being used to support reports, even college dissertations." She waved her hands about a small room whose walls were covered with black and white blow-ups of cemetery sites. Several photos revealed the African T shape, a marker that was to guide the spirit to the higher world. It looked like a Christian cross but the cross bar was longer and rested atop the vertical bar. The etching in the stone was too old to make out any shape.

"It's sad that modern African-Americans see these as simple crosses. They weren't." She stroked the photo as though it was the actual object. "They were part of the life cycle, cosmos worship that came from the motherland."

I don't know why that last statement surprised me except that I hadn't heard Africa referred to in those terms before. Of course, it was the motherland, and I shrugged it off as my own ignorance.

"We've got several dissertations and articles being written on the subject." Olivia moved to a table in one corner of the room. "These are drafts. Our experts are taking a look at them." She brushed her hands across the bound work as though blessing it. "And here," she pulled out a file drawer, "are photos taken of every single site we have proved is real." She pulled up one picture of a flat square space surrounded by shells and broken pottery. "The archeologists had to dig around the grave to find these border items. That's also a part of the African religion. The graves need a border and there must be nothing on top." She tapped the grassy area.

"Part of the belief in the spirit movement?" I asked.

"Yes. We have a booklet. You can read it if you like." She pulled a slick pamphlet from a box of several just like it and handed it to me.

"And Preacher Billy," I said, "where does someone like him figure in all this?"

Olivia frowned. "I don't like to speak ill, you know. I mean his spirit is part of the cosmos, too." She sighed. "He represents a more modern world, post slavery, but very much in the realm of Christianity. It's an African brand, all right, but it doesn't reflect these ideals." She waved her hand about the room. "He tends—tended—to place fear in the hearts of his congregation."

"Isn't that what all religions do? I mean, isn't that how they scare people into going along with their beliefs?"

"Fear of what happens after death, you mean?"

"Just that. If you're scared enough about where your soul is going, don't you lean on the preacher, the shaman, the priest, even the witch doctor, for guidance?"

"I suppose. But these old cosmos ideas are more peaceful, almost a transcendental cycle of life belief."

"Gospel music, shouting 'amen!' are not a part of that?"

"Nor are ghosts, and Billy did his best to keep that belief alive." Olivia's eyes turned to anger. "If you can't put the fear of God in them through shouting sin into a microphone, then tell them the haints are out there to get you while you sleep in your bed at night."

I nodded. Inside I told myself no wonder there was total disagreement between these two camps. Olivia might have been at home among the sixties gurus, while Billy wouldn't have been able to stay quiet and still long enough to sound an "om."

"Now that Billy is gone," I tried to avoid saying no longer a hindrance, "what do you expect will happen to your preservation work?"

"It will go on, as it would have had he been alive. I know someone will take his place in that church in the woods, and his followers will turn him into a martyr for a while. But maybe for a few moments, I can have the ear of the commissioners and the trustees all to myself." She looked at me and smiled, a Cheshire cat grin if ever I saw one.

"Did the sheriff come and see your collection?"

"Yes. Detective Amado seemed quite interested in the place."

"He questioned you at the same time?"

"Somewhat, but he wants me to give a statement at the department. I plan to go there later today."

"He asked where you were at certain hours, I suppose," I said as I moved toward the door.

"He did, and wanted to know if anyone could back me up." She smiled. "That's a tough one."

"Tough? You mean you were alone and can't prove it?"

"No, meaning I was not alone—at night. I don't want to prove it as it could embarrass someone." She shrugged and smiled a broad grin. "But what's a little embarrassment in this world?"

CHAPTER FOURTEEN

All the way home, I thought about Olivia's words and wondered who had been sharing her bed. Her soft, secretive way of speaking made it clear she wasn't about to tell me. Tony Amado would be another story. It suddenly hit me. Amado, with his clean cut and stylish clothes, his groomed hair, and Latin good looks, would be just the sort that Olivia might favor. I laughed out loud. Tony would meet his match with her.

Plato sat at the bottom of the steps and barked his welcome. He ran back and forth between the two men who sat on the top step and jumped around like he hadn't seen me in years.

"What did you tell him?" I asked. "He's too excited."

"Just scratched his ears and told him to wait for his mama," said Pasquin. "Edwin threw him a stick until they both got tired of it."

Edwin grinned underneath a heap of orange material. "I got vests for us all," he said.

After dishing some dog food for Plato and making sure he had water, I left with Pasquin beside me and Edwin in the back seat, surrounded by his quilted vests.

"Are you going to tell us what this is all about?" I asked.

"Don't quite know yet," said Edwin. He gazed out the window as though riding in a car was something new.

"Been pretty scarce in his talk lately," said Pasquin. "He's been what the kids say 'freaked out' by finding Billy's body."

"I need to see what Marshall has found out about that. The community is going to want to give the man a funeral soon."

"Yep," said Pasquin, "and that one is going to be one big show." He looked at me. "You're going, right?" Which meant, of course, "you're going to take me along."

"I'll let you know when and where," I said.

Edwin leaned forward and guided me toward Becker Road. His breath, hair, and clothing put out a kind of clean gamey odor, not offensive, but definitely Edwin. Instead of pointing with one finger, he used his entire hand, sort of like military hand signals on a ship.

We crossed the county line at one spot only to cross it back into our own county again. After two small paved lanes, we hit a dirt road that had tire tracks from hunter's trucks.

"Park here," he said, and I pulled the Honda station wagon beside a truck with high wheels.

As soon as we got out of the car, Edwin ordered us to put on the orange vests like some kind of teacher with kids on a field trip. We didn't ask where he got the vests, but they nearly swallowed all three of us.

"If them hunters don't see us in these, they must be blind," said Pasquin, laughing and slapping his straw hat back on his head.

We took a trail that had signs of recent walkers, most likely hunters on their way to the tree stands where they would wait for deer. I didn't want to be there when they returned with their trophies, smooth-haired, camel-colored deer with red holes in their bodies, hanging limp across the back of the truck. Such killing bothered my sense of decency.

"It's through here," said Edwin. He turned onto a side road. The earth was soggy here, obviously leading to the edge of a stream.

The stream turned out to be a fairly wide one, and from the dark color, it appeared deep enough to hold fish and other water critters. Edwin led us down the side of the water until it widened even more, and the banks on each side grew higher.

"Now let's stand up here," he said as he led the way across a newly constructed wooden bridge that rose high off the sides of the banks. He stood in the middle and looked over the railing. Pasquin and I did the same.

Below us, the dark water appeared clean. At the sides, there were lily pads and fallen tree branches, but no algae grew on top.

"It's not stagnant," I said. "That's a good sign for this area."

"Water's moving," said Edwin. He pointed to the center of the stream where indeed the water did seem to take on motion, almost like someone had turned on a natural spring spigot.

The reason for the flow soon became obvious. First the eyes, then the bumpy hide of an alligator moved to the surface. He raised his entire body to the top and with slow motion, swished his tail in the water until he was directly beneath us. We looked down on a still, almost docile gator of nearly five feet.

"See how he noticed we were here?" said Edwin. "See how he came and stopped right here beneath us?"

"Don't tell me you have secret powers over alligators as well as snakes," I said.

"No. Somebody's been feeding this alligator. Tossing food off this bridge. He got used to it and knows to come this way when humans stand here." He leaned over to make sure the animal was still there. "Yep. Somebody's been feeding him."

"You haven't tossed any food to him, have you?" asked Pasquin.

"Not me! I'd never do a stupid thing like that." Edwin frowned at his friend. When he looked back at the gator, his frowned changed to puzzlement. "But somebody has."

"Stay here," I said, and moved off the bridge to the shore line. It was a high bank, but the gator would have no trouble shooting up it if he thought I had food. I was hoping he'd stay tuned to the men above his head.

I walked the shore on both sides, looking for tracks or signs that something had been tossed into the water. Finding nothing on one side, I crossed the bridge and searched the other shore. Still nothing revealed that any human had been around the area.

"Hunters wouldn't be that foolish, would they?" I didn't doubt that someone who sat in a tree stand all day, gulping beer, and never seeing a deer, might toss the rest of his lunch into the stream. Hunters would know better, but that didn't mean they'd do better.

I went back to the top and looked over at the alligator, his full body still waiting in the water for a handout. No wagging puppy tail or hassling tongue, just there in full view.

We waited in silence, wondering when he'd get bored and move on, when suddenly a voice came from the far side of the bridge.

"Three orange pips on a bridge," said a low voice. It came from a huge man, both in height and girth. He had on camouflage and an orange vest like ours, only his fit tight and barely closed in the front. He carried a rifle in one hand.

"Do you hunt here often?" I asked.

"Every year," he answered and stood the rifle on its end, leaning it against the bridge rail. "And you?"

"We came to look at the alligator," I said. "Have you seen anyone feeding it from the bridge?"

The big man moved to the edge, causing the new boards to groan. "Damn thing is waiting for a handout, isn't he?"

I waited for his answer.

"Never seen anybody give it anything. They'd be stupid to do that. Damn thing could go after you when if you traveled next to the water."

"Do you build campfires?" asked Edwin all of a sudden.

The big man laughed. "Not hardly. Scare the deer away."

"There's a campfire spot over there," Edwin said and pointed into the woods.

The big man followed his finger and started walking in that direction, carrying his rifle now at his side. We followed.

"Show me," he said and let Edwin lead us into the trees.

The tree line was narrow because another stream pushed through behind them. At one spot, where they was a clearing, someone had stacked rocks. Signs of a fire showed up in smutty debris in the middle of the rock circle.

The big man leaned over and stared at the cold rocks. He moved farther and began to sniff the area.

"Nothing cooked in here," he said. "It wasn't used to fix food." He reached for a dead branch on the ground and poked around the smut and some wet ashes at the bottom. "Looks like somebody came here to burn something." He pulled up a cloth that had been partially burned. "Clothing?"

I took the cloth by the tip and held it up to the sunlight. It was silky with a purple flower print on one edge. "Like material for a woman's dress," I said.

"Why'd somebody want to burn their dress?" said the hunter. "Who are you people?"

I answered him by pulling out my cell phone and calling Tony Amado. He told me to tell the big man to stay put.

On his way to the area, Tony had phoned Folsom, the deputy, and asked that he meet us there. Folsom Senior, Junior, and grandson came at once, followed by Tony and Vernon. As soon as they had seen the fire pit, Tony called for the techs. Marshall Long was going to have to navigate a footbridge.

The big hunter leaned against the tree and picked his teeth with the toothpick he kept behind his ear. His gun leaned against the tree with him. He showed no urgency to leave.

"Never know who you'll meet in these woods," he said once as I passed him.

"And who have you met here?" said Loman who had been sent over to take his statement.

The man began to recite his history with this hunting lease, a long and fond one, from the occasional kid who didn't know how to handle a gun to hunters who drank enough to see polka dot deer in their dreams.

When the tech van arrived, Marshall already had on his white coat. He handed his kit to an assistant and grabbed hold of the bridge railing with both hands. He was as big as the hunter but a lot less confident in bridge builders.

"Don't say a word, Miz Luanne. I'm here to rescue you." He moved up and over, almost walking sideways until he reached ground where he sighed relief. "I need to work in a big city."

"And miss all this nature?" I said.

"Where's the hole?" He frowned at me, but followed as I led him into the trees.

Tony and Vernon leaned over the pit. The Folsom family stood at the edge of the trees. All three had acted surprised that someone had built a fire here.

"We don't check this end of the property often," said Junior. "It's open for hunting long as the man has paid his lease, has a license and follows the rules."

Old man Folsom moved from one position to another, complaining that his joints were killing him. His grandson, the deputy, stood with hands on his hips, glowering at Tony who had taken control of the operation.

"Like three old buzzards," said Pasquin.

"When it gets dark, they'll look just like those birds in the trees on the river," I said.

"Dark is coming, too," said Edwin. When the three of us stood together, the others must have commented that we looked like three squashed oranges that had fallen from a tree.

We heard Marshall grunt as he bent over with a long tweezer instrument and pulled up more cloth. He looked at it with a light, then tucked it inside an evidence bag.

"Plenty of it here," he said. "Most partially burned, but some still intact. Flowery. Solid blue. Striped." He commented on each as he placed them in separate bags. "Could be you've called me out here to identify somebody's garbage." He spoke to no one in particular.

I pulled Vernon to the top of the bridge and told him to look over the side. The alligator was still there, his full back exposed to us.

"Edwin says this is an indication that someone has been feeding it."

Vernon nodded. "He's probably right. Full exposure like that, waiting while humans are all over the place. He expects food."

"Well, he's not getting any unless Marshall topples over the rail."

"That would be more than the gator could hold," said Vernon.

Marshall took his samples back to the van, treading carefully across the boards again, while his assistant held the bags. He stood at the back of the van and loaded them in their place.

"We finished the exam on Preacher Billy," he said. "Nothing spectacular, unless you call a blow on the head spectacular. Done with a rock. There were pieces of stone and dirt in the wound."

"And the rest of him?" asked Vernon.

"Remarkably healthy for a man his age. No sign of artery or heart disease. Not even diabetes." He tucked the bags in place and turned back to us. "You know, he must have been out there deliberately. He had on jeans and a shirt and jacket with running shoes. Now, I doubt he went jogging way over in the swamp, far away from his own house and church. He was in the woods, probably right where he wanted to be."

"At the slave graveyard—or what we think might be one," I said. "Olivia Jourdain overheard us talking about it, and I know she told him."

"Why would she do that?" asked Vernon. "She wanted him to stay out of their debates on site preservation."

"Why indeed? She had a motive, I'm sure."

Tony and Loman moved to the top of the bridge and let Edwin show them the lurking alligator. The critter was still there, ever hopeful.

"How deep is this stream?" asked Tony.

The hunter, who had edged himself across the bridge and placed his rifle in its holder in his truck, turned back. "It's pretty deep in places. Gets fresh water from an aquifer and sink somewhere back in the woods. Kids used to swim in it. Big fun to grab hold of a rope strung across one the overhanging oaks and fly over the water and drop down. Has to be deep enough for that."

"Kids better not do that now. Looks like that gator's expecting food"

The hunter grinned, his jowls pushing nearly back to his ears. "Swimming is out of season. Too cold now, and the kids are back in school. Any swimming will be done in gym pools."

"Gym pools?" said Loman, his half-open eyes twinkling. "How come they didn't have them when I went to school?"

"Figured you'd drown on the spot," said Tony, not cracking a smile.

Tony moved across the bridge and stopped Marshall before he got back into his van.

"What do you make of the burned material?"

"Making something of it is impossible right now. If I had to guess—and I figure that's what you want me to do—I'd say it's from a woman's dress or blouse, a man's shirt, and possibly a silk tie."

"Dressy clothes, then?"

Marshall nodded. "Not your normal romping in the woods outfit, nor a hunter's camouflage. Yeah, maybe prom clothes? Two kids come out here on prom night and strip. Go through some kind of ritual of burning the things, then hump in the bushes and swim with the gators."

Tony didn't laugh. "And end up in a gator's belly. Or, at least at the bottom of the stream." He glanced towards me and Vernon. I stiffened at having to dive with that hungry gator waiting at the surface. "Might have to call out gator trappers before we look for anything."

Pasquin moved off the bridge, pulling Edwin by his orange vest. "I thought the prom was in June. It's fall out here. Sounds more like Sunday-go-to-meeting clothes to me." He gently shoved Edwin in the direction of my car. Edwin seemed mesmerized by the hovering alligator.

CHAPTER FIFTEEN

I hate funerals. I'll do anything to stay away from them. At least the one for Preacher Billy would be partly surveillance. Tony and Vernon would go, both in plain clothes and on duty. I planned to take Pasquin. He wouldn't miss it, but Edwin wanted no part of it. The sight of Billy lying on the ground with his head smashed in, eyes wide open, still haunted him.

The local papers gave the upcoming rites all the publicity it needed. Besides being an unsolved murder, it had happened near a possible slave grave site, and a long way from Preacher Billy's church.

"Motive?" Most reporters began with this question. The sheriff was asking it, too, and so far, the only argument Billy had was with the historical preservation people, in particular, Olivia Jourdain.

"She had no reason to murder him," I said. "She resented him, was embarrassed by him, but to bludgeon him on the head with a rock in the middle of the swamp? I doubt it."

"Besides, she has an alibi." Vernon smiled and winked at me. The lovely Olivia had been discussing some historical work with a graduate student late into the night. All night, in fact. They went to breakfast at a campus cafeteria the next morning.

"She could have had him followed," said Tony. "Killing for hire carries the same penalty."

"Hire?" Loman glanced at his boss. "Wouldn't a killer for hire use a gun?"

"All right," said Tony, his jaw working in frustration. "Suppose she had him followed to see if he found any other sites. The person following got found out and retaliated with the rock."

We all shrugged.

"Let's get this funeral over with," I said.

Pasquin and I arrived early. He knew the crowds that would come, and he didn't want to be left standing outside. I wore a black pants suit, but it looked downright sporty in comparison to the throngs of women in black silk dresses with matching hats.

We joined the crowd and slipped into a pew next to Olivia and her niece. Both wore black dresses and an African print scarf tied loosely at the shoulders. The orange and yellow print stood out against the expensive suit material.

"Who are the two women with children?" I asked when I saw the same two women who were with Billy at the fish fry.

"His daughters," Olivia whispered. "The kids are his grandchildren."

"No wife?"

"Left him years ago."

When the choir walked in from the wings, each member wearing a black robe over a white shirt or dress, the packed church dropped its whispering and started chatting louder.

"It's open coffin in spite of the head wound," I said.

"Always is," said Pasquin. "We'll have a chance to view the body when the service is over."

"Oh, boy," I said. I hoped the funeral director had done something good with the head wound. Somehow, looking at bodies in a coffin is worse to me than seeing them murdered on the ground.

In the background, the organ player pounded suddenly on the

keys and began a rhythmic introduction to the choir. The members stood in three lines, swaying in unison to the music. When the singing began, it was no mournful dirge from the Middle Ages. It was near rock in beat and decibels. The congregation stood, feeble old ladies helped up by young men. Some shouted "Amen!" over the music; others joined in with the choir. There was lots of hand raising and open crying.

The preacher, a young black man who looked a lot like Billy, stepped to the podium and began talking about a man he called his uncle.

"Uncle Billy knew the value of life, knew the hardships of it, the insults, the sometimes hopelessness." Shouts of Amen! punctuated each noun. "But he never gave up. He led people, kept them in the arms of hope for a better world, both down here and up there." The preacher pointed upward, and the entire congregation looked up, hats and heads moving together.

The preacher held nothing back. He began to sweat, and his voice grew hoarse. He loosened his tie and pranced back and forth across the raised platform. On two occasions, he returned to the podium and read lines from the Bible, mostly about resurrection. He finally got around to speaking of Billy's manner of death. It was a threat from God, that all killers would feel retribution, and he prayed it would be sooner rather than later. The congregation stood and roared their approval.

The choir began singing again, almost dancing in tune with the passionate gospel. The preacher joined them, his voice loud and leading.

Olivia sat stiffly, holding the hand of her niece who was equally stiff. I glanced at them, then at Pasquin who smiled and tapped a rhythm on his knee. He enjoyed this. I felt bewildered, engulfed in a cultural scene in which I had no role.

"See what I mean," said Olivia. "This kind of behavior bothers me."

I looked around at the open weeping, the clapping, the shouting.

"Looks like it works for them," I said. "It must be a way to release the grief."

Olivia shot me a frustrated expression and said nothing else.

It finally came time to view the body. I grabbed hold of Pasquin's arm as he led me into the line. I looked back and saw Olivia head out the door with her niece. She wouldn't look at Preacher Billy.

I tried to view the crowd as I moved slowly down the aisle. It was mostly black, people Billy knew in his community, but the few whites who were there seemed to be local country people. Life and history had certainly played a part here.

The choir swayed and sang as we approached the casket. I could see the outline of Billy's face just above the rim. At one moment, I thought of looking away, but the fascination drew me in and I saw his puffy head lying on the white silk. He wore a black suit and held a Bible in his hands. Instead of makeup or fake hair, the undertaker had placed a hat on Billy's head, a classy one like men wore in the forties. They had managed to adjust it so that the brim stood out stiffly and the wound didn't show at all.

"That was clever," I said as Pasquin and I went outside and joined the masses of people on the lawn. Many of them had not been able to find seats and listened through the open doors and windows.

"Your friend took off early," said Tony. He and Vernon had stood near the side doors during the entire service.

"I don't think Olivia approved of the send-off," I said.

"Or didn't want to look at a dead man," said Tony.

"What happens now?" I asked.

"Cemetery," said Pasquin. "We can't miss that."

I groaned. All I wanted at the moment was to head to Mama's Table and eat as many fried shrimp as she could muster.

We rode behind a long line of cars to a large cemetery gate about a mile from the church. The graveyard near the church was full from years of funerals. Billy would get a big place in the middle of a newer facility.

The green tent top covered the dug hole. It seemed there were people for miles around the site where pallbearers placed the shiny coffin atop the lift. The choir, still in robes, gathered around and sang without accompaniment, still swaying and nearly dancing to their rhythms.

The preacher did his part, shouting out the "ashes to ashes, dust to dust" lines and saying a good-bye to his Uncle Billy.

Pasquin and I stood back from the scene. It was, after all, grief that belonged to someone else. Tony and Vernon were at opposite ends of the area. Reporters with cameras filled in the edges near the parked cars.

When the emotion was finally over, people drifted toward their cars. Women had taken off their big hats and were fanning themselves with the brims. Men were loosening ties and carrying suit jackets across their arms. The crying and shouting had stopped. Mourning spent, it was time for more immediate needs.

"Lots of photographers," I said as I walked toward the car.

"Even one back in the trees," said Pasquin. He had stopped and pointed toward the tree line. A solitary man stood there with a camera.

"Funny place to be," I said. "The other reporters are over here."

"Might not be a reporter," said Pasquin. He continued to stare.

I left his side and strode against the crowd toward the tree line.

The man was young and slightly built, but he was too far for me to see his face. When he realized I was coming his way, he let the camera drop on the ribbon around his neck, stuck some glasses on his face and turned into the woods.

I took off running. It was going to look a little strange to all those people behind me, but I didn't care.

Once I entered the woods, I stood still, listening for the movement of brush or the cry of animals. Nothing moved. In the distance, a car engine started and tires squealed. I wasn't sure where I was, but I might find something where the car had been parked. I took off running again, this time beating back limbs and stepping in moldy leaf piles.

The trees ended and I found myself on a dirt lane. A car had been here, all right. The soil was sandy and the imprint visible. I called Vernon on my cell phone. He wasn't that far away. He and Tony had seen me running and had followed.

"Could be nothing, but I'm taking no chances," said Tony. "Get the scene techs out here and get a cast of that track."

While we waited, Tony and Vernon skirted the area, looking for footprints along with more tire tracks. The few prints near where the car had been too messed up by the runner to get anything. But the tech got a good cast of the tire track.

"No way you could have glimpsed the car, Luanne?" Tony said, his eyes accusing me of not running fast enough.

"I didn't even know one was there until I heard the engine start."

We made our way back across the cemetery to the cars. The place had cleared out with the exception of the preacher. He rested against a car, his robe folded on the hood. It looked as though he'd smoked half a pack while he waited.

"You'll end up with Uncle Billy pretty soon if you don't quit that habit," said another man, a pallbearer.

"Yep," the preacher said, taking a long draw on a fresh cigarette.

When we approached the cars, the preacher joined us.

"Find anybody back there?" He nodded toward the woods.

"Nobody," Tony said, not about to give away he had a tire print.

"Might have been a reporter just using the other side," said Loman. He was breathing heavily. Running after people through the woods was not one of his talents.

"Might not have been," said the preacher. "Look, the guy was white, right?"

Tony looked at me.

"Seemed to be from a distance," I said.

"Could this be, well, racial?" The preacher threw down his cigarette and stomped on it.

"If it is, we'll see signs of that and go after suspects in that area," said Tony, clearly becoming agitated. "Right now, we have to look at all angles." He stood up straight and looked the preacher in the eye. "Do you have any idea, however small, of anyone with a grudge against the preacher, racial or otherwise?"

The man looked bewildered now. He shook his head before he spoke. "Uncle Billy was good to everyone, all races. You saw the white farmers who came today. Nobody wanted him dead."

"Nobody, except the one who hit him on the head," said Tony.

Pasquin waited in the car, fanning his face with the straw hat he had left on the back seat. We followed Tony and Vernon to Mama's Table. It would be a respite from a troubling day, but also a place to confab over the situation.

Mama's Table needed painting. It was the favorite eating place for the fishermen along Fogarty Spring, its landing offering a tie-up for any boat that could navigate the Palmetto River. We parked near the front door on a thin layer of gravel.

Mama said she'd been aching since the morning, her knees giving her fits. She was a heavy woman and years of traipsing about a kitchen and dining area had pressed one time too many on the cartilage there.

"Doctor says I need to have the left one replaced soon." She took a seat on a rolling plastic chair near the table where we sat and waited for fried grouper.

"You have any help back there?" asked Pasquin and pointed to the kitchen.

"Yeah," she laughed, her chubby face showing just the hint of aging lines. "Tulia came in to help when she heard about my knees."

Tulia was a sporty old lady who had helped me out once when I had a bout of poison ivy. She was a fixture, a member of the swamp brigade, and rivaled Pasquin for knowledge of events that happened among the cypress and moss.

"Not much of a cook," said Pasquin.

"I swear, old man, I'd have to close up if she hadn't come this morning. I went into town for a shot, and that just eased it up a bit." She rubbed the knee, exposing her large thigh.

"No fancy serving," shouted Tulia as she entered the room with a big pan full of fried fish. "And I didn't get around to the hush puppies. You'll have to eat white bread."

"Forget the bread," laughed Vernon. "You've got enough corn-meal on these filets to make up for bread.

Tulia's thin red hair had turned gray in some of the strands. It all stood up as though being pulled by an electrical force from the ceiling. Her sharp nose pointed out and down from piercing blue eyes.

"Sit down, old girl," said Pasquin and pulled a chair to the table.

Tulia had a seat and leaned over to shuffle sauce bottles and a bowl of grits toward us. "Oops! Cole slaw." She jumped up, headed back to the kitchen and returned with a mixing bowl full of fresh slaw.

"Must not be a thing wrong with your knees," said Pasquin. He sprinkled hot sauce on his fish, while the rest of us settled for tartar.

"Nope. Knees are fine. Back gives me a twinge or two sometimes." Tulia had poured herself a glass of tea and sat away from the table to sip it.

"Funeral was pretty big, I imagine?" said Mama.

"Way too big," Loman said. "Hard to find anybody suspicious in that crowd."

I turned to Tulia. "Have you ever heard of a grudge or hard feelings against Preacher Billy?"

"Hah! He sure weren't no angel when he was younger."

Vernon toyed with a piece of fish. Under his breath, he said, "She let loose with a ton of salt." Mama overheard him and whispered back, "Sorry."

"Quite a cutter, was he?" I asked

"More ways than one. His wife ran off with another man. But Billy got to them somewhere around Quincy and did a little cutting with a knife. Didn't kill him, and the man took off before charges were filed. His wife lives out in Texas, I hear."

We stared at each other. The salty fish lay uneaten in our plates. Tulia hadn't put enough cheese in the grits, and the cole slaw had been made with sour cabbage. Things were not right with the universe.

"Make a note to check out the ex-wife and this guy who got cut," said Tony. "When did this happen?"

"Years ago!" Tulia gulped her tea. "Those two girls were still in school. But," she leaned toward the table, "I hear his wife is not an ex. She never bothered with a divorce, and I don't guess he did either."

"Easy enough to check," said Loman, adding it to his list.

"And question those daughters again." Tony frowned now, mostly at the food.

Tulia moved closer to the table. She grabbed a piece of fish from the pan and took a bite.

"Wondered why ya'll weren't eating this stuff. Guess the ocean was too salty where that came from."

CHAPTER SIXTEEN

A class in the Germanic roots of English did not have the impact of a beloved preacher's funeral. I gave the lecture, met with students, and looked for a place to find a coffee. The weather had taken on a definite chill since Billy's demise. I guessed all the warm air had risen into the cosmos with his spirit.

The small coffee shop with its three outdoor tables was doing mostly take-out business as students grabbed their lattes and headed for class. I sat at one table and pulled my sweater close to my neck. The sun shined in this spot and if a wind didn't pick up, I'd be warm enough. I drank my hot brew, stronger than I remembered it from a few days before, and thought about the woods with the slave graves. How young would those people have been when they had to be put there, I wondered.

"Miz Fogarty," a voice nearly as cold as the weather interrupted my thoughts. "Would you get a coffee for me?" Reena leaned over in her wheel chair and tossed a couple of dollars on the table in front of me. "They don't seem to be waiting on people today."

I took the money, asked what she wanted and went inside. She had pulled her chair to the table when I returned.

"Stay awhile," I said.

That seemed to make her happy. Her body visibly relaxed in the chair.

"My friends have abandoned me," she said. "I guess people

get tired of dragging an invalid around. It's fine as long as you're healthy, but if you become a burden, look out!"

"It would seem that with four people in the same department, at least one could go to class with you."

"Same department?" She took a sip.

"You're all anthropology majors, right?"

"Just me and Carl. Lily and Dalton are in biology."

"Biology? I guess I assumed since they were on the Folsom tour, they had the same interests in school."

"Nope. Those two are trying to finish pre-med courses. They spend a lot of time in labs. It's that jerk, Carl, who could push me about, but he makes himself scarce most days."

"I understand he's going to do a senior project in morgue lingo." I tried not to laugh, but Reena caught my expression.

"He's fixated on the subject, I think. He should be in biology with those other two—speaking of the devil."

The sun was shining bright now, and as I turned, it flashed briefly across Dalton's glasses. Two shining objects pointed at me, showing no face or eyes behind, like a flaring moment of two light bulbs. Then it was dim again, and I could see Dalton moving to a seat beside Reena.

"Ladies," he said. He looked at Reena without saying more.

"I'm fine, Dalton," she said, wasting little good humor on him. "I'm learning fast about this wheelchair stuff."

"It's good for you to be able to help yourself," he said, his voice timid. He winced when she stared at him with a killer expression.

"Such friends I have," she said.

I had been watching Dalton. He leaned close to Reena, touching her arm twice. She jerked it away twice. He didn't say much after his summation of her chair condition.

"Miz Fogarty," said Reena. "Will you be diving in the pond again?"

"No. It's not even a pond anymore. It has been delivered of all the water in an effort to find more bones."

"Rain will take care of that," said Dalton. He touched Reena's arm again. She stared down at it, then lifted her eyes to meet his.

"I hadn't realized you and Lily were biology majors," I said and sent off a spark that caused Dalton to jerk his body towards me.

"Yeah, pre-med," he said. He stared first at me, then back at Reena. I got the feeling he was unhappy that she talked about him.

"Forgive me if you find this intruding, but won't your eyesight affect your career?"

Dalton put his fingers to his face and barely touched the rims of his thick glasses.

"Shouldn't. I can see fine with them." He laughed and said, "Provided they don't fall off during the operation."

"You're planning on being a surgeon?"

"Maybe," he shrugged. "My interest lies more with the dead that the living."

"You can say that again," said Reena, who was now toying with her empty cup.

"Forensics. Pathology. That sort of thing," he said, ignoring his friends' cynicism.

I leaned forward. "Is that where Carl found his interest in morgue lingo?"

Dalton's eyes appeared to grow bigger behind the glasses. "Interest in what?"

"Morgue lingo, the special language and terminology used by people who work in morgues and the funeral business."

"I didn't know he was doing that." He looked to Reena, who refused to look back at him. "I know he's interested in old burial sites in the USA, but that other." He shrugged.

"He chose linguistics as his senior project," I said, "with this particular topic."

Reena glanced toward her friend, took a deep breath and said, "Miz Fogarty, there must be tons of books on this subject. You know what I think? I think Carl is going to compile a bunch of terms from several of these books and hand that in as a senior project. I can't see him spending real time with coroners and funeral directors."

"Oh, Reena, you don't know him if you say that." Dalton glared at her. "He's fascinated with the dead. He's still jumping for joy about those bones we found."

"Must be nice to be able to jump. I seem to have forgotten how." Reena winced when she tried to turn her head away.

"Does your back hurt?" asked Dalton.

"Oh, no. It feels like pure bliss." She straightened and tried to put her hand in the small of her back.

Dalton placed his hand on her arm and held it tight this time. "It will get better, completely well, in fact." He stood up and checked his watch. "Gotta run. I'm helping in the lab today."

Reena looked at me after watching Dalton cut across the grass and disappear behind a building.

"Helping in the lab? Ha! In his dreams."

"What do you mean?" I asked.

"He's barely passing his courses. He's not going to make it to med school, even if he graduates biology." The scowl on her face made her look old.

"That's too bad," I said. "He seems like an intelligent fellow."

"It's those glasses. People equate thick glasses with bookishness. He'd rather read space comics." She smiled, her cynicism making it to the table.

"Space comics? You mean like comic books—the old Flash Gordon stuff?"

"That and a lot more modern stuff. His apartment is stuffed full of those things."

"Where does he live, by the way?" I wasn't sure she'd tell me.

"South of campus. He's got a little old house that's been there for ages. It sets back from the road under some trees. Tiny little wood frame thing with one bedroom."

I knew the type. The university had once been surrounded by frame houses like that because students needed housing. The houses tended to be old with bare essentials, and as the university grew they were torn down with a vengeance. Few were left, their land replaced with block-long university buildings. If Dalton had found one, he was lucky.

"And where do you live?"

"I share with Lily. It's a modern box in a building. We've got a lower floor, thank goodness. My father set up a temporary ramp when he was here."

I looked at the young girl, at the age when she should be doing the things campus life offered. Instead, she was bound to her wheelchair.

"Aren't they having you do any exercises for your back? I mean, do you get on your feet at all?"

"I try. I make it to bed and to the bathroom. It's easier in the chair for everything else." She didn't look at me. Was it guilt for not trying harder or giving up on herself?

"Have you been to counseling?"

Her head went up and she stared at me. "You seem a bit nosy today." The change in attitude shocked me.

"Only concern, Reena. I was there when you fell, remember?"

"Yeah, well, I'm handling it, okay?"

"Enough said." I raised my coffee cup in a salute to her privacy. Gathering my papers, I stood and was about to say good day to her.

"Miz Fogarty." Her voice took on a little girl quality, vulnerable this time. "Could I call you sometime?"

I stared at her. The sun glared off the metal of her chair arms. Pulling out a business card, I placed it in her hand. "Anytime," I said. I didn't want to become her counselor, and the back of my mind told me to set up defenses against a barrage of calls. I felt pangs of guilt all the way to the car.

Driving down the long paved highway and onto my lane into the swamp, I kept thinking about Dalton. There was something about him that didn't set well with me. He seemed concerned. He even seemed smart. Reena said no to both.

Before I reached my house, the cell phone rang. I stopped in the middle of the road to answer.

"We're diving the stream," said Vernon. "It's pretty small, and really needs only one diver. But, it's got gators, and the rule is dive with a buddy." He hesitated. "Want to be my buddy, little girl?" He made his voice sound lecherous.

"In a stream?"

"And any other place, ma'am."

"If I have a choice.... Look, like you said, there are gators in that stream and at least one who expects to be fed."

"Tony's contacted the gator hunter who'll get that creature out of there first."

"And when do we do this dive, and what are we looking for?"

"Early tomorrow morning, bones, clothing, stuff like that."

"In other words, just about anything?"

I prefer to sleep in on Saturday mornings, but this time, I agreed to tank up and look for human remains in a dark, probably grass thickened, stream bottom. "Only for you, Vernon," I said.

When I arrived the next morning at the bridge, Tony, Vernon, Loman, and some deputies were standing back, their eyes on two people with ropes and hooks stacked on the bank.

"Can someone stand on the bridge?" The man called to the group. He was lean, rugged, with the once light skin that had been permanently weathered by lots of sun. The woman next to him had the same look, only she tended to smile, forcing the leathery skin into rows of crows feet around her eyes and mouth. Her hair was cut short and bleached a bright yellow.

"You go, Luanne," said Tony.

"Gee, thanks. Female food is better than male, I assume." I walked to the top of the bridge and looked over the side.

The alligator wasn't far away. I heard a splash and in a few seconds saw small wakes in the water. When the gator reached sunlight, his hide shone black in the light. He slowed his pace and rose to the top of the water. Floating at the edge of the bridge, he waited for me to drop food. Instead, he got a barb in the top of his head and a rope around his powerful jaw.

He was not a happy gator, but the hunters had him tight and dragged him on shore. Before the critter's tiny brain could thrash in its own defense, the man was sitting on its back and holding the rope around the mouth. The woman stuck duct tape around its jaws with the speed and precision of an elf on Christmas presents. The man moved backward and pulled the animal's feet up far enough to tie them with wire. The only thing the animal could use as a weapon now was his tail, and the two humans knew how to avoid that. They lifted him into the bed of their truck.

Tony moved forward and signed a paper for the man. It was a

necessary operation, a dangerous animal that had learned to eat
from humans, and had to be removed.

"Where will you take him?" I asked.

"Alligator farm about ten miles from here," said the man as he
waved. He sat in the passenger seat. His wife revved the engine
and drove through the trees, the specimen of a primitive ancestor
resting silently in the back of the truck. Alligator farm meant he'd
become fried gator meat one day. It was the old law of the jungle
irony: who feeds whom.

"You ready to suit up?" Tony asked. I stayed on the bridge for
a while, waiting to see if that poor gator had any friends who
would come for a handout. None showed. I headed for the dive
trailer.

Vernon and I entered the water at the bottom of the bridge.
The plan was to search one side of the stream as long as it was
deep enough, then move to the other side. The others would station themselves along the bank, guns ready, in case other gators
decided to take revenge.

The water felt cold as though a fresh aquifer fed the stream. I
figured there was a cave in here where the water would be pushed
through, keeping the area clear of algae. Underneath, the stream
bed made a vee, the sides of the banks continuing down until
they met in an abundant growth of grass. The strands waved back
and forth in the wake of the running water, and tossed side to
side when we swam over it.

The sunlight barely reached the grassy bottom, and we had to
use our head lights as well as hand-held torches. The lane was
narrow. I gave Vernon the lead, and the two of us moved slowly
up the stream like catfish fumbling for scraps of debris on the
grass blades.

The stream was what a pristine swamp waterway should be,

and that was rare. Fish swam among the grass, and a few snails clung to foliage. They would attract the anhinga birds. And the life cycle would go on as ordered by the universe.

We continued upstream, and I assumed the ones on the banks were moving along with us. The water was shallow enough to send bubbles to the top. When we came to a shallow spot, we literally had to stand up and move across to deeper water. As I suspected, the cave showed up, a narrow slit about a foot long and just as wide. No diver would ever get inside, but the cold water shot out of it like someone had turned on the tap full blast.

I shined my light into the opening. The limestone cave walls quickly gave way to total darkness as the opening turned toward the depths.

We swam back to the bridge and took a break.

"Nothing down there," said Vernon. "Not even a tiny bone."

We put on the masks again and moved to the other side of the bridge. The water still moved, pushed by the force of the aquifer, and the grass waved as we passed over it with the lights. The stream finally tapered off and there was no more room to swim.

Vernon and I returned to the bridge area. He pulled off his tank and passed it to Loman. I tread water beneath the bridge and took a look upward.

"There," I said. "Isn't something on the side, a discoloration?"

Tony retrieved his powerful sheriff's issue flashlight and aimed it at the bridge, just where the under support boards met the walk-way. "Get Marshall out here," he said.

CHAPTER SEVENTEEN

"Flesh," said Marshall. "No doubt about it. We'll have to do some tests to know if it's human. Don't see any blood."

Marshall had been a sight when he rested on one hip atop the bridge and leaned over sideways to scrape his sample from the board. A photographer had taken some photos before that, and the poor man had been recruited to hold onto Marshall's big waist in an effort to balance him. Once the specimen was in the bag, it took two people to pull him from the floor of the bridge.

The next day, we met in his lab office. He handed over the preliminary report to Tony, and moved to a table where packages of dark material lay on top.

"These are the pieces of cloth pulled from the fire pit. The flowery stuff is probably from a lady's dress, the cloth is a man's shirt, and this," he held up the third package, "is part of a man's tie."

"Just as you suspected," said Vernon. "What's the meaning of it all?"

"Even with the partial burn, it's got a residue." Marshall turned the packages over and back again. "There's a fresher powder on each item. That's something undertakers put on bodies to, shall we say, deodorize prior to the service." He stopped and looked at us, his tiny eyes glowing mischievously in the chubby face.

"During the viewing, you mean?" Vernon suppressed a grin.

"Even after that, the body resting in a grove of flowers at the preacher's feet." Marshall tossed the packages back on the table. "But that's not all."

He picked up the shirt remnant bag again. "This one had a residue of melted plastic and drying compound." He looked up and grinned. "Want to hear what that's all about?"

Loman shifted and winced.

"Looks like you're going to tell us," I said.

"Sometimes, when a body has to have an autopsy, the undertaker will fill the body cavity with a drying compound to absorb moisture. And, if it's particularly—shall we say necessary—he will use a plastic garment suit around the torso before dressing the body for the funeral. Whoever wore this shirt, had that done."

"The man may have had an autopsy right here?" asked Tony.

"Could be, or he could have had it at a hospital. Sometimes they like to find out the extent of a disease or the family wants it done."

The room remained quiet for a moment. My head filled with a scenario, one that brought us back to the task at hand.

"Burned burial clothes, flesh on the bridge, an alligator that expects food to be thrown from the top." I took a deep breath. "Could someone be feeding dead people to gators?"

"We didn't find any bones," said Vernon. He hesitated before adding, "Could someone be removing the flesh and tossing it to the gators? Maybe taking the bones elsewhere?"

"Like to old grave sites?" added Tony.

"If we get DNA from the flesh and if it's human, we'll try and match it to the little we got from the bones," said Marshall. "But, I'd say you've got the profile of one strange dude running around that swamp."

"It's time to pay a visit to the Folsom's," said Tony. "We'll all go." He turned to Loman. "Get Deputy Folsom on the phone and have him meet us at the Folsom home, the old man's home. He's the only one who actually lives near the bridge. And tell him to make sure his father is there, too."

We rode packed into a patrol car, Loman at the wheel. Marshall stayed behind. He'd be on call if anymore body parts surfaced.

Loman skirted down a major highway and pulled onto another paved road. Several houses skirted the edges, sitting back among trees, their dark corners able to hide any sort of bizarre habits. Soon, the houses gave way to nothing but trees and flat, sandy earth. Loman turned onto the dirt road that would take us into a heavy forest and finally to a partial clearing. A double-wide trailer sat in the middle, a big mound in the back that let us know it was septic tank country out here. It would be years before city sewage was installed.

We pulled up beside a sheriff's car and two battered trucks. Gerald Folsom paced the deck someone had built in front of the trailer, a cigarette hanging from his lips. Butts on the deck floor said he'd been there and filled his lungs while waiting for us.

"My dad and granddad are inside," he said and held the door for us. "Find a seat anywhere."

Old man Folsom had what he needed inside his big living room. A sectional sofa, draped in a drop cloth, faced a huge television set. He flipped it off when we arrived.

The three Folsoms took a seat on the sectional and faced Tony and Loman who had pulled some dining chairs to the living room. Vernon and I took opposite ends of the sofa.

"We got a sticky situation here," said Tony. "We think somebody has been using your property to feed humans to gators." He waited for a reaction, the darkened television screen behind him like an ominous black cloud.

"We let hunters use this side of the land," said the old man. "Can't stand out there and give tickets."

"You do take tickets for the walking tours, however. What kind of people have been on those tours lately?" Tony nodded toward Loman who was using a pencil on a tablet.

"Mostly like what you saw the day we found the bones," said the old man. "Locals, college kids sometimes, families."

"Ever get people who are doing histories of the area?" I asked. This seemed to startle the men, and all three heads turned my way.

"Yeah, sometimes," the old man finally said. "Some local authors who want to write about the background. Even some history professors and such. I don't think they believed much of what I said."

"You mean," said Vernon from the other end, "no one believes you actually have a volcano out there?"

"No!" The old man nearly shouted, and his son grabbed his arm to calm him down. "People have fun with that legend, and nobody ever tries to find out if it really exists." He jerked his arm away from his son. "What I'm talking about is the slave graveyard stuff. We've had people, of both races, come to look at the stones."

"Did Preacher Billy or maybe a woman named Olivia Jourdain ever take the tour?" I asked.

"Both did. Separate times. Billy brought a whole bunch of his congregation. They weren't interested in the volcano rocks, just the grave site. Later on that woman came. She was with a black man who had an accent so heavy I couldn't understand a word he said."

I looked at Tony. "Her African ex, perhaps?"

"Was there ever any indication that they drifted over this way, farther into your land, and possibly onto hunting grounds?"

"If they did, I didn't know about it," said the old man.

"Have you ever done a thorough search of your land?" He turned to Deputy Gerald Folsom who looked as though he needed another cigarette.

"No," he shook his head and shifted on the sofa. "Had no need to and besides, that's a lot of acres to search. You find something here, something else could appear where you'd been."

"Just the same," said Tony, "it may have to be done. We'll wait for the lab reports to be sure what it is we're looking for."

An air of tension prevailed inside the trailer as we stood to leave. Clearly, Gerald wanted to be in on the detecting, but his ownership of the land put him in a suspicious light. He made no protest.

I took a quick look around the room before walking out with the others. The living room connected openly to a dining room and kitchen, separated only by a breakfast bar. A few empty beer bottles rested on top. The one end table next to where I had sat, was a cluttered mess of junk mail and a TV remote. Beneath the remote, one letter with a first class stamp looked out of place. The return address was the historical society.

"Do you correspond with any of the historical agencies in the area?" I asked.

The old man moved to the end table and snatched up the letter. "Forgot about that. It's just a request for them to do a study."

"And will they?"

"Well, maybe. It's just they want to do the study alone, exclusive rights, so to speak. Don't know if I can grant that."

"May I see the letter?" Tony said.

The two men stood in a silent stare for a moment, until old Folsom realized it wasn't to his advantage to say no. He flipped the letter in his hand and gave it to Tony.

"Keep it," he said. "With all this trouble, I'm not letting any history people roam around my land."

"Good idea," said Tony and stuck out his hand to shake the old man's. "I'm leaving a card. Let me know if you think there's anything else we need to know."

Back in the car, we pushed together and bumped along the road to the main highway.

"Funny how the son never says much of anything," said Vernon. "The old man did most of the talking. The deputy didn't seem of much use, either."

"A search of that land is in order," said Tony. "Make a note to call the judge soon as we get back."

Loman nodded, probably in a quandary as to how he'd make a note and drive at the same time.

"On the other hand," said Tony, touching the steering wheel. "Let's check out the original site while we're in this part of the world." He pointed to a turn-off, and Loman took it on two wheels.

"What do you plan to find there?" asked Vernon.

"No plans. Just curious." He looked at Loman. "Call the office on your cell when we get there and get the ball rolling with the warrant."

We parked in the clearing where the Folsom Walking Tour sign stood like a ghost. Someone had placed a piece of typing paper with a magic marker note that walks were temporary postponed. The first rain would smear the message. Already, morning dew had caused some of the letters to weep.

Yellow scene tape crisscrossed the opening between trees, but we ducked underneath and trudged onto the trail where old man Folsom led us to the volcano.

"Stay on the path, but look for anything that might suggest

visitors," said Tony. He led the way, his creased pants and stiff shirt not picking up even a nit.

Loman followed. He kept trying to shove the notebook and pencil into a shirt pocket that was already too full of pens. He stumbled a few times, and was covered in nits.

"Here's the volcano," said Tony. He looked at the pitiful mound of burned rocks and laughed. "And people believe that?"

"Want to believe it," I said. "You'd be surprised how many people's lives are just too boring. They look for these things."

We moved on to the edge of the wooded grave site. Here, more yellow tape surrounded the hole where Reena had fallen. The area was a mess of mud and dirt now from the search.

"Look!" I said and pointed to the bottom of the pit, deeper now than it had been excavated for more bones. "There's a white rose in the bottom."

We all leaned over to look. Vernon shined his light onto the flower, a perfect specimen.

"I don't think these things grow naturally in the woods," he said. "I'd guess someone just recently tossed this into the hole."

We passed the infamous log, the so-called hanging limb for the poor kid who had put a rope around his neck years ago. The oaks around it had grown old and sturdy, sturdy enough to hold another body.

"They're more here," I said as I wandered into the main site area. "Someone is treating this like a memorial." I wasn't sure if it was Preacher Billy's people or Olivia herself or maybe even Jensen, but I knew someone was going to be questioned. Tony's eyes flared with anger against anyone who would violate the scene tape.

"What an ugly hole," I said as we approached the holding pond, or what was left of it.

The dredge had removed most of the water. Only a few puddles stayed on the bottom, and they were covered over with new algae growth. It had taken over the damp banks and sides, too, like some outer space invader that planned to smother earth.

I spied the area in the bank side where I'd found the skull caps. Algae made a thin curtain over the dugouts now.

"To think we actually dived in here with tanks a few days ago."

"More flowers," said Tony and pointed out some strewed white roses just above the area where the skull caps were found. He walked over and picked up one. "No algae, mold, or aging signs on this. I'd say whoever put them here came by today."

We all looked around the trees, a bit skittish as to who may be watching right now.

"Let's talk to Jensen." Tony turned and headed out of the forest and into the white cemetery behind the church.

Jensen sat in a chair outside his trailer, his face turned to the sky as though he needed the sun's essence for life. He didn't hear us until Tony spoke to him.

"Damn! Oh, sorry," he said. "It's just that I didn't hear anyone approaching."

"Could it be that you don't often here people approaching?" asked Tony.

Jensen stared at him. "Not sure what you mean. I was asleep just now."

"I mean," Tony stared down at him, "could anyone come through this way to the grave site and you not hear them?"

Jensen looked around, his eyes confused. "Not if I'm out here, but then maybe they could. You just did. Now, if anyone comes in the night, I might be watching TV or sleeping." He stood up, fully awake now. "Look, I'm not the watchman for this area. I don't even own a gun should a trespasser cross your tape. If you want a patrol, then put one here."

"Did you spread white roses on the graves and in the bone sites?" Tony took a stance meant to intimidate the tall reverend. In his support, Vernon and Loman stood behind in the same stance.

"White roses?" Jensen laughed. "Not hardly." He looked around his little yard. "There are no roses growing around here, and I assure you, I don't buy flowers."

"What about members of your congregation?"

"The church ladies bring flowers every Saturday evening for Sunday service, but they never go into the woods, not even into the area of the graves unless they've got a relative buried there."

"Have the Folsoms been around?" I asked, and all four men turned to stare at me.

"Not to my knowledge," he said. "But they stayed off church property even before all this."

"So no one has been out here to your knowledge?" Tony's black eyes stared at the man's blue ones.

"Just that historical person, Miss Jourdain. She came to chat, however. I gave her tea inside. It was a bit brisk that day. She never went into the woods." He appeared a bit flustered as though talking about her made him nervous.

"And what did she want?" asked Tony.

The Reverend Jensen looked away, a slight grin on his face.

"At first, I thought she was interested in finding out about the slave graves. She even gave me some literature about the markers they used and the old African religions."

"At first?"

"Not sure what she ultimately wanted," he grinned. "But she very nearly got it."

CHAPTER EIGHTEEN

"Miss Jourdain seems a bit of a seductress." Vernon had retrieved a camera from the patrol car and was snapping the white flowers. I followed him into the woods. Tony and Loman stayed with Jensen. They had mentioned something about attending one of his sermons next Sunday.

"Seductress with a motive would be my guess," I said. "She's a beautiful woman, and I'll bet has resorted to using her feminine wiles to get what she wants in this world."

"And what does she want?"

"A bit of power in her department. A say-so in this historical preservation stuff." I looked around at some of the prints in the soft earth near the empty pond.

"Vernon, were there kids in this area?"

"Not during that fish fry. They didn't go past the white graves."

"Those prints would be gone by now. Look. All these tiny foot prints around the edge."

We leaned over and took in the countless prints of a child's size foot. They seemed to be of the same shoes, but almost like dancing, or running, about the edge. Vernon adjusted the zoom to take a picture.

"The only child I can think of right now is Olivia's niece." I lay a ball-point pen next to a print.

We sat in the car as a cold drizzle of rain had begun to fall. Jensen retreated into his trailer as soon as he'd confessed to a bit of necking with Olivia. He hadn't seen the niece since the Halloween fish fry.

"We'll have to pay a visit to Miss Jourdain," said Tony. He frowned.

"I'll go if you don't want to," I said.

The car remained quiet. Tony, I was sure, had been attracted to the lovely Miss Jourdain. It wouldn't sit well for him to imagine a bit of groveling about between her and the big Scandinavian preacher. He sighed.

"Maybe that's best. She might say more to a woman."

I knew this wasn't true. Olivia would more likely open up to a man who would take her to dinner, buy some expensive wine. This wasn't going to happen here. Tony, with all his good looks, was awkward and a bit selfish with most women.

We drove to the end of my road where I asked to be dropped. I would walk the three-quarters of a mile. The rain had stopped and the sun sent out an almost vertical orange glow as it set. It had always been a pleasant walk during the fall of the year.

Barking greeted me in the form of Plato who came pouncing down the road. We frolicked about with some sticks until he got bored or distracted and headed into the bushes. I kept moving.

The cell phone rang in my jacket pocket before I rounded the bend to my front door.

"It's Folsom, the elder," said Tony. "Just got a call they found him in the woods near his trailer."

"Dead?"

"Not yet. Banged over the head, it seems. We're heading back that way. I want you to call Olivia right now. Try to get her to meet you somewhere tonight."

It was an order, though not one I had to obey. I was an adjunct diver, not a deputy. I smiled. It was nice to be treated as such by a boss who was mostly reluctant.

I headed inside. The living room was cool enough to build a fire. In my kitchen, I searched for things that could be used to entertain and found a nice tin of shortbread from Scotland, still unopened. And I had a box of oranges that I knew would spoil before I could eat all of them. After I made the call to Olivia and got her promise to come by for an after dinner chat, I sat down to peel the oranges. I planned to cut them into chunks, toss in some coconut and a few grapes, to make Southern ambrosia.

It seemed a bit strange for Olivia to agree to come out here, late at night. I stopped peeling a few times to ask myself why she didn't want to wait until I saw her in her office.

"Whatever," I shrugged. "Maybe she wants to see how I live."

The fire was going good when the lights showed on the lane leading to my house. Olivia brought a bottle of wine, something I hadn't thought of when I made a pot of hot tea.

I placed the bowl of ambrosia on the coffee table along with some serving dishes, and the plate of shortbread.

"Would you like tea or do you prefer the wine?"

"Oh, tea, of course. You keep the wine for some special dinner with a special guy," she said. Her smile was wide and her eyes a bit hazy. I figured she'd already had her wine or was swimming in an afterglow of something pleasant.

I poured our tea and served her some of the fruit.

"I need to talk to you, Olivia, and I think it's best you tell me what you can about seeing the Reverend Jensen."

She took a bite of orange and coconut, smiling again. "Good stuff," she said and put the dish on the table. "The Reverend had some good stuff, too."

I waited. Olivia stared at the fire and smiled. She seemed to have some nice thought on her mind.

"What did he serve?" I asked.

She jumped slightly. "Not food."

"What then?"

She looked at me, her eyes glazed and happy. "Do you smoke, Luanne?"

"No, I never got the habit…" I stopped. Her expression told me what I needed to know. "I see. You and the Reverend shared a little…"

She held up her hand, still smiling. "I'll never tell. We had a nice chat about the grave site. He thought we could negotiate something with the Folsoms about preservation."

"He talks to the Folsoms?"

"He wants to. You know, people who take up the ministry and act as guidance to people, often have skills to help in other areas, too."

"I'll bet. Kind of like your wide-variety-of-skills-Renaissance-man?"

"Whatever do you mean?" She turned a coy face to the fire. "The reverend is a gentleman in every aspect of the word."

"I see. He never started anything with you? Anything physical, I mean?"

"He? Let's say he never completed it."

"Olivia," I leaned forward and poured more tea for both of us. "The night you visited the Reverend, did you bring any white roses?"

She looked at me, her lips pursed as though on the verge of laughter. "However did you know?"

"Did Jensen know?"

"Oh, no. I didn't have them for him. Dandy bought them. She

wanted to place them on the graves."

"And did she?"

"I think so. She traipsed about the area while I was talking to the reverend."

I stopped to think about this situation. Olivia was inside a trailer, dragging on weed and cuddling with the preacher, while her niece romped about in the dark among graves, dropping white petals into holes.

"It sounds like a dangerous thing for her to do."

"Not Dandy. She's too familiar with sites that I've taken her to all her life. We've got a kind of little cult of our own, one we invented. I feel if I talk to the spirits, drop flowers, and generally feel good around the graves, they won't haunt me."

I stared in disbelief. "Olivia, you're sounding a bit like Preacher Billy."

"No, no! He believed in harmful ghosts, things that would spook you and cause bad luck. Dandy and I have a kind of earth goddess attitude. Death is calm. It doesn't rise up to scream at you."

"Well, you've answered my question about the flowers. Why did you allow Dandy to go inside the scene tape to drop flowers?"

She shrugged. "I told her to stay in the white graveyard but she must have decided the other spirits were more akin to hers."

"And where is Dandy tonight?" I had visions of the little girl turning three circles in the moonlight and sprinkling sweet water on the ground. Plato would come along and circle with her, barking at each arc in the holy dance.

"She's with a sitter," she said.

"She's your niece but she lives with you?"

Olivia glanced at me, again the mischievous twinkle flashed my way. "Not really. She's mine. The product of a misstep one night with a friend I met before my first marriage. It was just convenient to call her niece and not daughter."

"I see." I was right. Olivia would use whomever she needed to arrive at her own goals. Had Preacher Billy lived, even he may have been outfoxed by this woman.

Olivia straightened her legs and crossed them. They were the long graceful legs of a model that matched her tall body. "Men, no matter what the race, seem to be the ladder to success," she said. "I'd like that not to be the case, but I could spend a lifetime trying to change it." She grinned at me, picked up a piece of orange with her manicured fingers and popped it into her mouth.

"I decided to use, rather than abuse, the situation."

"And where do you want to go with it?"

"Not sure yet. If I can get a few more promotions, I may try for something in politics."

"Politics." I nodded slowly. "Olivia, you do know that you're going to have to tell all this to Detective Amado when he questions people.

"Already have," she said. "Not the stuff about Jensen, of course. That happened later anyway."

"That's what I mean. You'll have to tell him you were inside with Jensen while your niece was romping around crime scene areas, spreading flowers."

She sighed. "Then I'll tell him." She stood up. "But, Luanne, you let me tell him. Our conversation here is between us females."

I said nothing. I wouldn't reveal that it was Tony who told me to conduct this interview. He'd get an earful from me whether she liked it or not.

"I need to get back," she said. "Sitter, you know." She thanked me for the refreshments, told me I was one brave soul to live out this far, and said her goodnights. "And by the way, join us Sunday.

Reverend Jensen does his pulpit justice." She smiled and waved a
good-bye as sweet as any Southern belle.

Standing on the screened porch, I watched her car's taillights
fade into the trees. It would take her nearly forty-five minutes to
return to her house. I went inside and dialed her home phone.

"Hello," came the light voice of Dandy. When I asked for her
aunt, she said she wasn't in right then and offered to take a message.

"May I speak to your sitter?"

"No, I mean I don't have a sitter. I'm old enough to stay here
alone." She must have suddenly realized she shouldn't have said
that to a total stranger. I heard a gasp.

"Don't worry, Dandy. This is Luanne Fogarty. And, you
shouldn't give away your situation like that to a stranger."

"Don't tell Olivia, please." It wasn't Aunt Olivia, just Olivia.

"No. She just left here. I'll catch her on campus tomorrow. We
won't mention the call."

Dandy was grateful. I was, too. I had just found out that Olivia
had lied about the sitter. She left her daughter by herself, and
contrary to Dandy's belief, she was not old enough to be there at
night alone.

"How many other lies, Olivia?" I asked.

The phone rang with my hand still on the receiver, sending me
into a startled jump.

"We're at the hospital," said Vernon. "Seems old man Folsom
got a bit angry with what's been happening on his land. His grandson said he stood up and mumbled something about taking advantage and slammed out the back door. When he didn't return,
the two others went looking for him."

"Don't tell me. They found him in the slave graveyard."

"Wrong this time, Luanne. They found him near the bridge.

There are signs of a struggle that weren't there before, and it appears the weapon was a rock."

"Do you have the rock?"

"Nope. Like the one that hit Billy, it's gone. If it's in the water, I'll find it tomorrow."

"Did he say anything?"

"Out cold. Still is. The doctors won't know for a while if he'll pull through. He had a hemorrhage of some sort."

Vernon said they'd be doing the scene extensively tomorrow and I should come by as soon as I was free.

The night wasn't going to cooperate and let me sleep. I called Pasquin.

"Oh, let an old man sleep," he laughed. No one stayed up longer than this old Cajun. "I do have a young'un trying to sleep. Only person I know who smiles when he has snakes in his dreams."

"Edwin is still there?"

"Wasn't until he said he heard something in the woods."

"Like what?"

"Said it sounded like a car engine at first. Then a screech kind of like an owl."

"Probably was an owl. What would someone be doing in a car at night in those woods?"

"Edwin says it's haints out to get swamp folk. I'm betting it's lovers parked way back where Papa and Mama can't find them with their pants down."

"You are colorful, Pasquin."

"Why're you calling?"

"It's Folsom, the old man. Somebody decided to knock him over the head with a rock just like Billy. I don't want something like that happening to you or Edwin, and the way you both wander, you could run onto someone who doesn't want you around."

I shuddered at remembering Billy lying there with part of his head smashed in. Folsom must have looked much the same. I didn't want to think about more familiar faces.

"We'll stop wandering, for now," said Pasquin. "Sounds like people are seeing something they ought not to see."

I said my goodnights and trudged upstairs. Vernon would be out most of the night. Our moments of mutual comfort were getting too far apart.

Outside, a frog had taken up a rhythmic grunt, his voice low and earthy, while his cousins sang higher and in unison. I moved to the chair by my bedroom window and stared out at the darkness. I'm not sure how long I sat there, but when the sensor light suddenly came on, I pushed the curtain aside and searched for the sight of the movement that had triggered the mechanism. Expecting to see a deer, I saw a more human shape, I thought, turn and run into the darkness. A flash in the light felt almost like a camera flash.

"Someone is there," I said, and debated on whether or not to report it. Instead, I called Pasquin again and told him someone was about the woods and to lock his doors. "I just saw flashes, like... oh, dear," I said

Those flashes were trying to tell me something, and my brain finally found the connection. I couldn't be sure why but the fact that sunlight had caught Dalton's glasses popped up in my head. The flash in the forest and now here.

CHAPTER NINETEEN

"I'll see you later tonight," I told Vernon on my cell phone as I drove to the university the next day. "I've got something to do."

"Your 'to do's' scare me, Luanne. What is it?"

"Sorry, you're breaking up." I shut the phone and concentrated on the city traffic. In my mind, I could hear the curse that would come from my not telling him. I couldn't. The hour was early, too early to prepare for my first class. I turned on the computer in my office and did a quick check of student addresses. I ran back to the Honda that was parked in a loading zone.

I skirted the campus, driving on a side street and away from student traffic. I edged the Honda into a parking space beneath a huge oak, its limbs nearly touching the top of the car. It would give me the cover I needed. An old house sat far back into more trees, but I could see the narrow stoop at the front door. A light shined inside the opaque glass square.

A lot of trees grew around the little set back house, but modernity graced the other side with a huge cement and glass apartment building. The only character it had was a balcony built out from each set of sliding glass doors. Some tenants had attempted to make a mark with hanging plants. Most left it as is, too busy with student activities to worry about decor.

Nothing happened at the door of the little house, and I knew I'd have to drive back to campus to meet my class. Just as I sighed and started the car, I saw a van pull up in front of the apartment building. A door opened on the ground floor and Reena wheeled herself out in her wheelchair. The man who bounded from the driver's side of the van helped her stand. He held her slightly for balance as she climbed into the passenger side. Carl Mabry then folded up the chair and placed it in the rear. Once back in the driver's seat, Carl sat in his without starting the van. Lily came running from the building. She carried a set of books, nearly dropping them when she climbed into the back seat.

I looked again at the house tucked among the trees. Dalton wasn't coming out, and I couldn't wait any longer. I followed Carl's van. He made the short drive to one end of the parking lot near the linguistics building where he pulled into an unloading zone for the handicapped. Reversing the chair process, he had Reena on the street in a matter of minutes.

I parked the car and did a walk/run to catch up with her moving chair.

"Would you like a coffee?" I asked as I came alongside.

We sat at the same table near the building. I had thirty minutes.

"You live near Dalton, right?"

She didn't answer, and I had no time for contemplation.

"You live in that apartment building nearby, with Lily."

"I told you before that I roomed with Lily."

"And Carl?"

"Same building, different floor." She sipped her coffee without looking at me.

"You said Dalton was a biology major. Any chance he interned, or maybe just worked, with a morgue somewhere?"

Reena looked around her as though she could grab help out of the air.

"What do you want to know?"

"Just what I asked."

"Morgue? No." Her eyes darted from me to her cup and back again.

"Then where?"

"He…" She stared at me, her eyes watering over as though she'd break into tears any minute. "I can't," she said. "I promised not to tell."

"Don't you think the police will find out? It doesn't take a lot to check someone's work records. And if they find out you didn't come clean, they will be rather unhappy."

"He and Lily worked in a funeral home for a while. They were just student employees. The funeral home hires students who might one day become undertakers. It gives them some experience kind of connected to forensics."

"Kind of? Yes, I guess it would."

"Look, I have to get to class. Try not to tell them I gave out this information." She pushed on the wheels and turned her chair abruptly, nearly bumping a woman carrying coffee take-outs.

"So do I," I said to the wind.

I had two hours between classes. Getting back into the Honda, I drove again toward the old house. This time, a red sports car sped past me in the other direction. The driver's glasses flashed in the sunlight. It was Dalton, heading somewhere away from campus, but also away from his own house.

I waited a few minutes, then grabbed a folder as a prop for being there and headed straight for the front door. The walk was full of leaves. Dalton didn't do much gardening. His flowers stood like broken sticks at the edges of the steps. I moved carefully. Some of the cement had broken, and the screen door didn't close all the way. I pulled it open and knocked on the front door. No one came. I tried to peer through the glass but its opaqueness prevented seeing anything but light, and that seemed to be off at the moment. Trying the knob, I found it solidly locked. I walked to the side of the house. There were no neighbors to watch me stand on my toes to peek into the windows. They were old, the sills peeling paint, and in some rooms, didn't close all the way. I leaned over to try and see through the slits. Dingy white blinds had been pulled down too far, but they couldn't hold in the scent of mustiness, a kind of rotten odor that crept outdoors. It wasn't unusual for a place like this to harbor mold, and given the lack of tidiness with some students, the smell might not be unusual. I moved to another open window. The smell was more pronounced in the back. It was like an overflowing garbage pail that needed emptying.

In back, there was another stoop to a screen door. This one was wooden and had rotted in several places. The screen door didn't work here, either. I slipped my hands into a pair of latex gloves and opened it. To my surprise, the wooden door behind it opened, too, its lock long gone. I found myself in a tiny sun room. A worn verandah lined one wall, its seat piled high with magazines and papers. The floor hadn't been swept, ever, it seemed. Dust lined the sill of the window at the end of the room. I knocked on the door leading inside the house. When no one answered, I tried the knob. It was locked up tight, just like the front door. This door had a window, too, but it wasn't opaque, just dirty. I took a chance and grabbed an old rag that lay on the floor and swiped it across the glass. If Dalton looked carefully, he'd notice this.

Inside, I could see a kitchen counter top, the old vinyl type. It appeared uncluttered, a surprise to me given the way the house seemed to be neglected. A stove rested on one wall, clear of any cooking pots. To the right, a rather large metal contraption sat a few feet from the wall. It's rounded top appeared to be like one of those outdoor cookers, only somewhat larger. I squinted, ducked down and tried to see what was on top of the cabinets. The smallness of the window blocked my view. Just as I moved to one side and tried to see further into the room, a noise sounded from the front. I jumped, turned and got off the porch as quickly as possible. Hiding in the trees on the other side of the house, I saw the mailman walk past with his mail cart.

I moved back onto the porch. Picking up some of the magazines, I realized they were a mixture of scientific journals dealing with the biology of humans, to forensic newsletters, to sensational stories that bordered on porn.

Back in the space behind the house—it couldn't be called a yard as it had no grass, only trees and leaves—I checked to make sure I left no footprints. At one point near the chain link fence that was invisible from anywhere but right next to it, I saw an old metal barrel. It had clearly been for burning, but the smut was old and reeked of its own kind of mildew. I stood on tiptoe and peered inside. The contents smelled of oil and rotting leaves, which looked like the entire mess was dissolving into a goo. On an impulse, I grabbed a handful in my glove. Removing the glove from the wrist and turning it inside out, I used it as an evidence bag.

"Marshall owes me one," I said. I tucked the glove inside a bag I found in my car and headed back to campus.

The day dragged on, and my rehash of the Anglo-Saxon linguistic invasion of the British Isles seemed to take longer than the actual event. The glove with the sludge rested on my desk. I didn't want to leave it in my office. It might begin to reek in the confinement of the latex.

"You want what?" said Marshall. He stood in front of me inside his office, the latex glove with its nasty little ball held out in front of him as though he'd never touched a dirty thing.

"Test it for something. I want to know what was placed in this drum I found."

"Something? You don't seem to have any idea what it could be. I don't do something." He thrust the glove back in my direction. I moved back, refusing to take it.

"You do 'something' all the time, Marshall Long, and you know I'm not handing you something frivolous."

"Where did you get it?"

"From a drum that had been used at one time to burn stuff, it seems."

"You said that already. Where is this drum?"

"In the woods." I stared him down, and he got the message.

"You planning on eating somewhere tonight?" He grinned. It was the inevitable bribe with this man.

"Wherever you choose," I grinned in return.

"Pick me up here at eight. I'll have to stay overtime to find just some preliminary stuff." He opened the glove and took a whiff. "Man! Not your garden variety perfume, is it?" He took a shorter whiff. "Familiar bouquet."

I wasn't sure if he was serious on that last comment or not. We agreed he'd tell me the results at dinner.

I sat in my car in front of the rosy pastel lab building. The hedges had been trimmed and the windows washed. If anyone really knew what went on inside, they didn't learn it from the outside.

"What's the latest on Folsom?" I asked Vernon, who was in the next county with Deputy Folsom.

"Still in a coma. If he pulls out, he may be able to say who hit him."

"Does his son have any ideas?"

"That's somewhat cagey," he said, and I could tell he was walking away from the other man. "Look, I can't talk now. There's something of a silent treatment I'm working on right now. Later?"

"I'm meeting Marshall for dinner. Can you join us."

Vernon promised to try, and I warned him not to pull Tony into this for now. He gave his grunt, disapproving but curious. I knew the signal.

A hurried trip home to change and feed Plato if he was around, brought me face to face with Edwin and Pasquin on my front porch. They sat in the rockers. Edwin's eyes were sleepy like he'd been there for a while.

"This poor fellow," Pasquin pointed to Edwin and grinned, "has been rightly plagued with goings-on in these woods." He nodded toward Edwin, getting him to tell his latest tale.

"I heard shouting in the swamp," he said, his eyes widening. "It came from back there where Preacher Billy was dead. I tried to do like Pasquin said and not call it a haint. It had to be real, so I just up and grabbed my shotgun and headed back there."

I gasped. The thought of Edwin traipsing into the swamp, looking for something human that could outsmart him, made my skin cold. I held my tongue and let him finish.

"I got back there, in the clearing. The voices were louder and just a-shouting at each other. A boy and a girl. She was slapping his face when they saw me."

"Slapping his face?"

"Like he was trying to make advances." Edwin nodded, and I nearly laughed at his old time interpretation. "When they saw me, they started kissing. He had her backed up against a tree."

"Did you say anything?"

"I told him to leave the girl alone, but they both laughed and said it was just a lover's quarrel. But I told them they couldn't do that stuff in those woods and to run along."

"And they did run along," added Pasquin. "When he told me about the incedent, I figured something wasn't just right. That area is too hard to find. Lovers would stay up by the river."

"What did these two look like?" I took a seat on a wicker stool next to Edwin.

"Kinda young. Light haired. Mostly skinny. I think they planned to have a picnic in the moonlight. There was a basket on the ground, one of those kind people use for sandwiches."

"Kind of cool out for a picnic at night, isn't it?"

Edwin grinned. "Saw it once before, when some people from the hotel tried to picnic and neck out at night."

"In the same place?"

"No, up near the Palmetto Springs Hotel, or just out from there."

"In the summer?"

Edwin nodded. He had put two parts of the puzzle together and guessed at the whole. I invited them inside, but Pasquin sensed I was in a hurry.

"Look," I said as they started out on the path to Pasquin's place, "I'm betting it was Carl and Lily, two of the college kids on the walking tour, who were out there. When they saw Edwin, they pretended to be lovers."

"He thought so, too," said Pasquin pointing to Edwin who had leaned over to hold a nice-sized frog in one hand. "He said it didn't look like the girl wanted to be kissed."

They drifted into the shadows, Pasquin telling Edwin he wasn't going to bring that critter into his house.

I grabbed a jacket and headed back to my car. If I broke the speed limit, I'd make it to the Net Makers, a seafood place that was a favorite of Marshall's. I was paying.

"You going to swing for the platter?" he asked. "I'm due for a platter—a giant one." Before I could say yes, he ordered it from the waiter, along with a beer and banana pudding for dessert.

"Vernon is here," I said as I saw his car pull into the lot.

"You want him to know this stuff?"

"He'll know what you know."

Marshall leaned forward and shook a plump finger in my face.

"I know something's afoot here, Luanne. And I'll bet you won't tell all."

"Just don't try to pump me, big man. You want a platter, you got a platter."

He leaned back and smiled. "And you might get more than you asked for, too."

It was platters all around. We dined on fresh fried oysters, shrimp, grouper, and dug into crab cakes. Cheese grits lined one end of our plates and a basket of hush puppies rested on the table. These were large ones, filled with onion. Cole slaw bowls rested beside the plates, the sweet cabbage tasting like home.

"Better than Tulia's?" Vernon asked. He grinned.

"Mama is going to have to improve her knees and get back in the kitchen," I said.

"Another beer," said Marshall, lifting his bottle to the waiter.

"What you got, old man?" said Vernon.

"Lots. And here's something to take to your boss." He fished out an envelope from his jacket pocket. "It's the findings on that scraping off the bridge." He leaned forward and tried to lower his voice. "It's human flesh, but because of the condition, we can't get any clear DNA strands."

"Just the elements would deteriorate it that much?" I asked.

"Not the elements. The boiling."

"Boiling?" Vernon and I shot each other glances.

"It's human flesh that has been boiled, most likely." He shrugged and popped a shrimp into his mouth. "Maybe somebody was cooking for the gator?"

This information made both of us look around at the other tables. It wasn't something anyone else needed to hear.

"So no DNA?" Vernon asked.

"No. Can't identify whose flesh it was."

"But," I said, "given the mortuary powder that was on the clothing, maybe the flesh was from the bodies."

"You're getting good at dinner conversation," said Marshall. "Want some more?"

We nodded, ignoring the platters that grew cold in front of us.

"That gunk you brought me from the barrel? I'm betting it's got some human flesh in it. Hadn't had enough time yet, but we're headed that way."

CHAPTER TWENTY

Vernon and I sat on my porch. We needed time together, and especially now with the new information. We both wore jackets to hold out the cold and stared at the open starry sky. It wasn't a moment to go inside for the warmth of a fire.

"You did something, Luanne." He rocked too fast, a nervous reaction to events that were crushing in on us. "I don't want to know what, but I'd like to know what you expect to happen next."

He would be a bit angry. There was enough of the traditional deputy in him for that, but he'd back off from expressing it. I had done too many things like this in the past that had paid off for him and Tony. If they didn't know, they could proceed.

Tony, of course, would have been furious and ranted at me before asking the very same question, "what next?"

"I suggest you find a way to get inside Dalton's house, and dig around the outside, too. I've heard that trash put at the curb no longer belongs to the occupant."

"How do you know he puts trash at the curb?"

"I don't. But I know he rents and must have a landlord somewhere. So do the other three who live in the apartment building down the street."

"Anything else?" Vernon smiled at me now and reached over to pinch my cheek.

"Might look into a mortuary job two of them had a few months back."

"You start it, we finish it," he laughed.

"Now just a minute. I've finished a lot of it, too, and sometimes at my own peril."

He stood and grabbed me up in his arms. "Stay out of peril, Luanne. I couldn't bear the thought of doing all this without you."

He felt good against me, and I folded my arms around his back. It was time to go inside and feel the warmth of privacy.

Predawn came with a telephone ringing on the chair beside the bed. Vernon rolled over and punched his cell.

I recognized it as a police call, but only paid attention when he sat up and groaned that he had to go. A quick shower and a cup of coffee and a second filled in a no-slip cup and he was out the door.

"Folsom is awake," he had said just before he got into the shower. "I'll call you about the other matter."

I was up, and it was too easy to justify another visit outside Dalton's house. I dressed in a warm sweater. Fall was getting into winter these days.

The sun rose between the trees lining the shabby street near the university. Some students were up and in running clothes, their young and supple bodies stirring up dead leaves as they jogged on the paved road.

The sports car was parked in the drive now. Dalton must be at home. I saw no light in the opaque window. Hunkering down, I sipped my coffee and waited.

The wait grew tedious. No one seemed in a hurry to get to class. I figured about half an hour before the first one, they'd come out of the buildings like ants.

A tap sounded on my window.

"We'll take over, Luanne," Vernon said, a frown on his face.

"Folsom couldn't say much, but he did ramble a bit about the 'young bastards.' That, and what you suggested, convinced Tony to agree to surveillance. But only that."

"He didn't get mad?"

"I didn't tell him the info came from you, but he guessed it." He looked about the street and smiled. "You weren't there. No one got scolded." He patted the side of the door. "But you have to go now."

I waited until he returned to his car nearly half a block away, then eased out of the parking spot and headed for my office. Manny pulled in behind me.

"How are the senior projects going?" I asked. The only one I knew about was Carl's. He didn't pick up on that right away.

"Nothing new in the world, is there? I wish they'd find an exotic dialect, or some ancient language that needs modern translation. How many times do I need to read about Navaho?" He expressed the tedium we all felt after years of the same thing over and over. It was new, and fascinating to the students—I remember wanting to spend my life with ancient Indo-European—but to professors of any age, it meant tiring hours of guiding student papers.

"And that kid who wanted to do morgue language, haven't heard anymore out of him."

"You might not," I said, and added, "he's like a lot of young kids—eager but not willing to work."

"I'll give a ripping if he doesn't do a project that I approved." Manny drifted into his office. His open door revealed a rather sweetish smell as though something from the sixties remained. Only incense, I told myself.

"I'll bet you will," I said quietly as I opened my own office. I sat in my swivel chair and gazed at the papers on my desk to be graded. Turning my back, I looked at the photos that I kept on some shelves behind me. Anyone visiting might think they were places where I had done linguistic research, a forest in Brazil perhaps. They weren't. I stared at Vernon and me standing beside a diving van at Palmetto Springs. We had fished out bodies from those clean waters. Another one showed us sitting on a bank near a stream where we'd found bones in the bottom of a sunken boat. It went on like that, a swamp, a dog, medical examiners, Tony and Loman, and finally a full body photo of Vernon in his bathing suit. His bald head and chest hair shined in the sunlight. He had been standing on my landing when I snapped the picture. The wide grin nearly sent me into orbit.

"Okay, Luanne, get to work." As though a savior appeared, my cell phone rang.

"This is against my principle," said Tony, "but go by and pick up Marshall and meet me at this address." I jotted it down. "And don't dawdle."

"Dawdle? Have I ever dawdled, Tony?"

I heard the click.

Marshall hated riding in my car. "It's just a toy," he said, but he climbed in anyway. His was in the shop.

"Okay, Candlestick Mortuary is at the end of Backgammon Road," I said and looked for the street signs. "Wonder why they named a road after a game."

"Undertakers play that to pass the time between customers," Marshall said. "Don't you know that?"

"Never learned that in school," I said. "I kind of thought it would be poker."

"There!" I turned onto a short paved road. A house at the dead end had been converted into a funeral home. It had the presence of a mortuary, large, looming, Victorian. A small sign out front, dark and dignified, gave the name. I parked beside Tony's car.

Inside, a receptionist guided us to an office where a Mr. Wise greeted us. Tony was already seated, and Wise offered us comfortable chairs and tea. He spoke in a low, deliberate voice.

"We've been looking into mortuaries, as you know," Tony explained to Marshall and me. "Mr. Wise here seems to have had three customers who might fit our description."

Wise frowned, not unlike Folsom when he heard someone had been hurt on his property. The threat of lawsuit loomed heavy in this town.

"You asked about three elderly people, one—a male—who had an autopsy before being prepared. Certainly, we have three such people just this week, but I'm sure many of the mortuaries in town would have the same."

"Did anyone named Dalton or Lily ever work for you?" I asked. Tony shot me a glance but shrugged it off.

"We often have people in here who work part-time," Wise said.

"These would have been students, biology students from the university."

"They'd have to also be going into the undertaking business to get a job here," he said. He pushed his nose into the air and eyed me like a Cheshire cat.

"Or at least said they were," I said.

Wise remained quiet for a moment. His mouth twitched. At the same time, Tony's jaw ground with tension. Marshall sat like a placid Buddha.

"We trust that people tell us the truth, ma'am," he said.

"Do people always tell the truth?" It was a rhetorical question. I didn't want to intimidate this man just now.

"Can you check your records?" asked Tony.

Wise brought in the receptionist who immediately recognized the names.

"Oh, yes," she said, "don't you remember, Mr. Wise, the young man with the thick glasses. When things got a bit busy, they brought in two friends on a more-or-less part-time basis."

"Reena and Carl, right?" I stared at her, and Tony stared at me.

"Reena, yes! An unusual name."

"They aren't going into the mortuary business," I said.

"Oh, dear. I'm sure they said they were."

"You don't check first?" asked Tony.

The woman fidgeted and turned to Wise for an answer.

"Sometimes we get busy and just need help," he said. He leaned toward Tony. "Sir, bodies require immediate action. It's expensive, and often unpleasant for the families, to let them lie around in cold storage."

Marshall looked away and smiled at Tony's grimace.

"Mr. Wise," I said, taking a chance Tony would let me question him. "Let me give you a scenario after which you can tell me how something can be done." I looked at Tony who stared at me with a threat in his eye. "This is just a 'what if' not necessarily a real event, okay?"

Wise looked nervous, but he nodded. His receptionist took a seat in the only other spare chair.

"If you prepare a body for burial, for a funeral, when would be the opportune time for someone to steal it prior to burial?"

Wise nearly rose off his chair, but sat back and swallowed hard.

"It couldn't happen."

"Never?"

He looked at the woman who gave him a disapproving glare.

"I suppose," he began, still looking at the woman, "that if the funeral were going to be what we call a direct burial, we wouldn't check the contents after it was placed in the coffin." He gulped again.

"And who would handle the coffin at that point?"

Wise didn't answer, but Marshall finally opened his mouth.

"Your hired help would watch over and transport the coffin from here to the church or grave site, right?"

Both Wise and the receptionist nodded.

"The coffin would have been sealed as soon as the body was placed there because the family wanted no viewing or open casket."

Tony sat up straight. "Let me get this straight. You've got students working on sealed coffins with no one checking what they're doing?"

"Now, now," said Wise, "we give them directions on what to do and when. Once they get that coffin inside the hearse, they are just escorts to the burial site. The grave diggers take over from there."

"By which time," I added, "the body could be removed and replaced with something of equal weight."

"How morbid!" The receptionist said in all seriousness. Had we not been almost adversaries here, we would have burst out laughing.

"Before we go any further, Mr. Wise, I want you to check your records of the type of bodies I mentioned and you said you had serviced against the hired help who worked on them. And, sir, this is ultimately police business. I expect an honest report." Tony waited stiffly for the man's answer.

We left Wise and his receptionist agreeing to get on it right away. Wise had broken into a sweat by that time. Funeral home scandal would ruin him, and it was always a subject of interest to reporters.

We leaned against the cars and chatted outside the Candlestick Mortuary for nearly thirty minutes.

"I see a disinterment coming," said Marshall. He rubbed his hands together like someone excited to get started.

"Even if it's only rocks in a sack that you have to examine once the coffin is up," I said.

"We don't know who to dig up right now, not to mention the mess it will cause with families." Tony leaned and paced and paced and leaned. "We have to eliminate other people in this, too."

"Miss Olivia Jourdain?" I said.

Tony stopped and stared at me for a moment, his dark Cuban complexion turning a bit red. "I checked her out today. She's at least got an alibi for the night Billy was killed."

"Jensen does funerals," said Marshall.

Tony grit his teeth. "Don't go anywhere!" He turned and rushed back into the funeral home.

"I told them to find out where the funerals were held, too." He shoved his hands in his pockets. "Got to be a sick preacher to remove bodies from coffins."

"I've seen sickies do just about everything," said Marshall. "Why not another one?"

"He doesn't strike me as the type to fiddle around with dead bodies," I said. "He prefers them live and female."

Tony stared at me again. I felt his resentment burn through me.

"Any reason for the Folsom family to want to feed humans to gators?" I asked, giving him an escape from the Olivia topic that obviously made him nearly pop blood vessels.

"None that we have found. I don't care for the deputy. I have a feeling he does some on-the-take work in his county, but I doubt he's into body snatching. And his daddy is a weary truck driver. The old man probably couldn't do something like that."

"And the Preacher Billy crowd?"

Tony shrugged. "No one under suspicion there."

"You know, Tony," I said, "Olivia told Billy about the new grave site. It was probably because of her that he went out there."

"I know that. I asked her about it, and she admitted she got him riled up about a site that was being kept from their community. She wanted him to see if it could be real, and then she'd take over from there. She said if it panned out, Billy would be grateful enough to trust her and listen to her."

I shook my head. "More and more, I wonder about Miss Jourdain's ability to analyze her fellow humans."

We left Mr. Wise's Candlestick Mortuary with him staring down at us from an upstairs window, his receptionist looking over his shoulder.

"Wonder if they share a bedroom up there," said Marshall.

CHAPTER TWENTY-ONE

I met Reena in front of her classroom the next morning. She had changed from the chair to a cane.

"Progress?" I asked.

"Yes, although my back gets tired quickly." She moved to a chair that sat in the hallway. "I have to rest often."

"Have you seen Carl or Dalton lately?"

She turned her face away and gazed down the hall. "No. They seem to have deserted me for healthier friends."

"Have they?" Why was she lying?

"Oh, I see Carl in class, and I might run into Lily once in a while, but I haven't seen Dalton in days."

"Don't you live near him?"

Reena, for a second, stared at me. "How do you know that?"

"I think you told me, didn't you?" It didn't ring true, but I meant to scare her.

"No, I don't think I did." Her eyes darted toward the class-room door. "I need to go in now."

"Why? That class isn't over yet."

She let out her breath in resignation. "I will see Carl and Lily on Sunday," she confessed. "They asked if I wanted to attend a service at that church." She caught herself and quickly added, "The reverend invited us, and since he visited me in the hospital, I felt I should go. At least one time."

"Good idea," I said. "Will Dalton go with you?"

She shook her head and visibly relaxed when students came pouring out of the classroom.

I watched her turn, stand with the cane and wait until the crowd gave her room to enter. Her movements were slow and a bit jerky, but she was clearly nervous about something.

When I finished the day on campus, I drove down the back street just to check the situation at Dalton's house. One of the cars parked nearby would have a surveillance officer, but I didn't focus on that. I slowed past the dirty wood frame tucked in an overgrowth of trees. The sports car was still not parked there.

"Could he have gotten wind of something?" I asked myself.

I headed for Fogarty Spring and the calm of a weekend. Vernon promised to come for the night if he could. The rest of the afternoon would be lazy, a respite from student papers and lying suspects.

With the weather turned back to an Indian Summer, I decided to take advantage of the few hours of daylight left. I took out my canoe, the gift from Vernon. Its red sides showed wear, a kind of nice patina from a lot of good times on the river. I shoved it off shore near the landing and hopped in, planning to go down river a ways and take a swim in a section of water with no grass.

In spite of the warm sun, the air was not humid and would feel downright cold when I emerged from the water. I rowed away from the banks and took the middle of the river through eel grass to clear bottom, a deep place where several aquifers shot fresh water up from great depths. Nearly a mile away, and out of sight of my house, I rowed the canoe next to a patch of water hyacinths and secured it there. Stripping down to my bathing suit, I rolled out of the canoe and into the water. The first cold shock nearly paralyzed me, but when my body temperature adjusted, I pushed beneath the surface and skirted around the clear area. The aquifers here made the water clear, with only a few strands of eel grass on the bottom. The water felt good now, and I surfaced and swam across the river. I wouldn't go into the heavy growth on either side, too many critters could be there, and I had no wish to encounter an alligator. I had already spied one on a bank a few yards back. He was doing his reptilian thing of taking the warm sun in preparation for a cold night prowl.

I floated, closing my eyes to the sunlight, and thinking of nothing. I had moved far down the river from the canoe, but I could still see it. Or could I?

I shot up from the floating position and tread water. The red canoe wasn't there. I swam hard back to the place where I'd left it. Battling with hyacinth vines, I dove under water to see if by some chance it had sunk. When I came up, I saw the pointed end of the boat nearly ten yards away. It was wedged between two cypress trees.

"This is not possible," I told myself. "I heard nothing." I had to remind myself that I'd been underwater and floating a long way from the boat. Someone had tried to steal it. Getting it back to navigable water wouldn't be easy.

I was in deep water, treading and tiring. Looking at both shores, I saw no one. Surrounding me was heavy growth and cypress knees. There was no other way to tackle this but to swim to the cypress and climb on the knees to pull out the canoe.

I watched for movement in the water as I slid through the lily pads, their vines grabbing at my legs. Taking hold of a cypress knee, I pulled myself up and lay on my stomach. Knobs pressed into my gut, a reminder that standing would be easier. When I pushed upward, I had to maneuver on the protrusions of the knees.

Balancing myself on a tree trunk, I pushed around to where I could see the entire canoe. It sat in water just beside the cypress growth but had become stuck between half-submerged roots. A pole rested in the water at the other end. When I looked close enough, I saw that it was a hoe. Someone had used that to try and pull the canoe to shore.

"He would have had to stand on the cypress roots to do that," I said, and looking at the area, I could see some fresh strips taken off a few of the knees. Whoever it was, wore shoes to do that.

I leaned over and lifted the canoe slightly and shoved it into clear water. Tracing my steps back over the knees, I dove into the water vines and swam to one side. Pulling it toward me, I tipped the side and rolled into it. When I had retrieved the oar from the bottom, I turned it around to head back to my landing. Something flashed in the spot near the cypress knees. I yelled, "Hey you!" my anger overcoming the need for protection. I heard running steps and saw fleshy legs head into the woods.

"It's not necessarily someone who's with this case," said Tony. I had called him from the cell phone at my landing. "It could be just some jerk who steals canoes."

"Funny it happens now and to me," I said. Tony's indifference always made me angry, and he knew it.

"I'll send Vernon to look. I understand he's going that way."

I ignored the last snide inference. It was typical Tony—imply that I was a hysterical female who had a sneaky affair going with one of his deputies. Deep down, he knew my value and knew the long-term liaison with Vernon was more than a hit-the-sack-once-a-week event. But voicing his cynicism was Tony's way of maintaining his superiority.

"And both of you show up at Jensen's service," he said. "If you can, get some photos of who's there."

"What are you looking for?"

"Just want to know if the man has attracted any of the participants in this bone fiasco."

I lugged the canoe to its usual resting place in my carport. Inspecting the bottom for scrapes, I glanced up, and found myself face to face with Edwin.

"Damn! You sure are quiet, Edwin."

He giggled. "Sorry, but I walk quiet around the woods these days. Even when your dog walks with me, I don't talk to him anymore."

"Why not?" I had visions of Plato wondering what this man was talking about.

"Too many killers about. If I talk out loud, they might know I'm there, and well, you know..." He stopped grinning.

"Is something happening again?"

"Mr. Pasquin is on the river in his boat. Couldn't find him, so I walked on up here."

He hesitated as though he had forgotten what he wanted to tell me.

"And?"

"Oh, I heard something strange for two nights and two mornings. A car engine and squealing tires way back in the woods."

"Which direction?"

"Toward the site I showed you. Where Billy was killed." He didn't blink.

"There are no roads into that area."

"Yes, I know. It's all brush and trees, but somebody has been running through it."

I offered Edwin some tea, but he said his boat was tied up at Pasquin's landing and he needed to tend to his pets. Snakes, to be specific.

I turned back to inspecting the canoe. When I found it un-damaged, I went inside and showered.

Warm and comfortable, I sat in the living room, tending to the trivia of life—bills and other mail—when a shouting came from outside.

"Miz Fogarty! Can you come out here?"

I hit the porch and nearly ran into Edwin who was coming through the open screen door. My first thought was that some-thing had happened to Pasquin.

"My boat! Miz Fogarty, somebody stole it!" Edwin almost danced around the floor. His breathing came in gasps from run-ning all the way back.

"Have you seen Pasquin anywhere?" I asked.

He shook his head. I took out my cell phone and dialed Tony, ready to throw a boat stealer in his face again. He sounded sur-prised and said he'd get Vernon on it right away. Then I dialed Mama's Table.

"Yeah, the old man's here. He's back in the kitchen with Tulia, trying to tell her how to make shrimp creole. Ain't going to work. She's a ham and eggs person." Mama laughed until she realized I needed her to be serious.

"Tell him somebody stole Edwin's boat from his landing, and that he needs to double secure his own boat when he goes home."

I sat on the porch with Edwin. He tried to drink a soda but seemed on the verge of tears. "It's not insured," he said.

"Your boat? Why not?"

"Never needed it."

"We'll get it back, Edwin. You'll see." I wasn't too sure, but I knew Vernon would try.

Vernon arrived with another deputy following. Both cars had their lights flashing but sirens off. After a few preliminaries of both incidents, he got on his phone and ordered a department boat to come down the river to my landing.

"Did you see anyone in the woods?" he asked Edwin.

When he got a negative, he said they'd go by river and look at both places.

I sat in the front next to the deputy pilot and guided him toward the cypress grove where my canoe had been dragged. Edwin sat behind me, next to Vernon, and his other deputy took the rear. The force of the powerful motor made wide wakes as we turned toward the area where I had been swimming.

"There," I pointed to the knees.

Vernon and one deputy climbed out, steadying themselves against cypress trunks, and walked across cypress knees sticking out of the water until they were able to climb onto shore. We watched them flash their lights about the ground.

"Definitely someone has tramped down the damp leaves there, but we can't find anything and they fade as they get back into a dryer area. Let's head for Pasquin's landing." Vernon took a seat next to Edwin, patting him on the shoulder.

"Not much effort to hide, is there?" said Vernon as held up a rope that had been cut. "Probably used a sharp kitchen knife." He leaned over to inspect the pole where Edwin had tied up. He found some fresh scratches.

"Is this the place Pasquin uses?" He asked.

"No, he uses the one closer to shore," said Edwin, pointing to the other side of the dock. "I always use this one 'cause I can climb out easier than he can."

Vernon looked around the road in front of Pasquin's house. Finding no footprints, he had the other deputy take down a description of the boat, with any distinguishing marks.

"You know what's on the side," I said.

"A snake?"

"He calls it Serpent Sally."

Both deputies smiled, but the one taking the data said, "Good. Helps identify it. Of course, let's hope the perp doesn't paint over it."

Pasquin arrived as we wrapped up the report. He was visibly shaken.

"I get my hands on him," he said, shaking his fist in the air.

"Don't even try putting your hands on anyone," I said. "I don't want to haul you off to the hospital."

The deputy who brought the boat called in the theft and was instructed to scout the river for a while. Vernon, his deputy, and I decided to walk back to my house. They would take the lead and look for traces of anyone running through that way.

"Why would someone take chances like that?" I asked. "I mean the boats around here are distinctive with their names and such." I grappled with a nettle that had caught on my jeans.

"Quick movement, I expect," said Vernon. "Needed to get away from here."

"The only way he could do that would be to go out to sea. If he tried to hide in a water lane, he'd be found pretty soon."

"Maybe that's all the time he needs. The department will look on the ocean, too."

Darkness engulfed the forest, and the deputies' lights darted about like some gigantic, nervous fireflies.

At the house, the deputy took the reports and headed back for the sheriff's department, but Vernon stayed.

"You got Tony's orders?"

"Going to church?" He stood over me, a serious look that broke into a wide laugh. "Can you stand it?"

"I went to a funeral in a church, didn't I?"

"This won't be anywhere nearly that entertaining."

"Entertainment. Now I never thought of church in that light. It's either shout at God or speak in such a monotone you put Him to sleep. I wonder what He thinks when the preacher shoves politics into the sermon?"

"Sighs and gives the man the finger, probably."

We both laughed and spent much of the evening playing house. He built a fire, and I broiled steaks. Plato came home and the two of them wrestled on the floor while I attempted to make banana splits. "Just like this hot and cold weather," I said. "Ice cream in front of a roaring fire."

We settled quietly. Plato napped on his pillow and kicked the air in some dream segment he was having. Vernon took my hand.

"Another thing we want to do," he said, "is get those college kids in front of Mr. Wise. Should be interesting to see that reaction."

"At the department?"

"Might be best to do it at the mortuary."

CHAPTER TWENTY-TWO

I refused to wear a dress. Vernon put on a suit and tie, and I decked out in a black wool pants suit that made me look like a political candidate. At least if I had to take off running after someone, I wouldn't snag pantyhose.

The church road filled up with cars again. Ladies stepped out, adjusted their skirts, and took off walking a few yards to the church door. Men followed, at least some men did.

"Do you see more women than men here?"

"Hasn't church always been filled with more women than men?"

Vernon took my elbow and slowed us down. He wanted to go in last and sit in the back where he could see as many people before the service began.

"I've heard that, but you'd think in a rural community like this, there'd be more men with the women."

We stood to one side as a van eased down the road. It wasn't parking on the side like everyone else.

"That's Carl Mabry's van," I said when I recognized the driver. Lily sat next to him, and Reena was in the back seat.

"Hey!" called Vernon and tapped on the window as the van slowed to let people pass on foot.

"Well, what are you doing here?" said Carl as he leaned across Lily. She smiled at both of us.

"I hope the same as you're doing," said Vernon. "If you're

219

going to services, park the van in that space." He pointed to a vacant spot in front of the long line of cars. "However, if you think you're going into those woods, you'd better back this up and head home." Vernon pulled out his badge and flashed it in the window. "Got it?"

"No woods. Jensen invited us, and..." Carl turned around and looked to Reena for help.

"You see," she said, leaning forward to repeat her reason for being there. "Reverend Jensen came to see me in the hospital, and I thought I should attend at least one service to respect that." Her pale face showed no expression.

Vernon stepped back and pointed to the parking space. Carl nodded and did as he was told.

Someone had opened the windows and let cool air refresh the tiny church. Up front, the ladies circle had placed a fresh, elaborate spray of fall flowers. On the table around the spray, they arranged gourds of all colors. It was, after all, close to harvest time.

The first two rows were packed solid with women of all ages, but mostly under forty. When the choir walked in behind the pulpit, it was still more women than men. The organist took her seat, spreading her choir robe gently over the bench. She was maybe all of twenty-five and smiled broadly when Jensen came through the door and stood in place.

"Strikes an image, doesn't he," I whispered to Vernon. We had deliberately waited for Carl, Reena, and Lily to take their seats. He wanted to be sure we were behind them in case they tried to leave.

Jensen's height made him tower over the pulpit as though he owned it. He wore a black robe over a white shirt and a white silk tie. His usually unruly, thick hair, had been tamed into a neat coif, thick and blond with only a hint of graying on the sides. His knock-em-holy look. He shined like a Norse god.

And all the women basked in his glow. I could see some of the faces from the side. They didn't take their eyes off him, and a blissful smile graced everyone of the ladies in the front. The ones in the choir weren't any different.

Jensen had been blessed with a voice, too. His deep bass boomed into the congregation when he sang along with everyone else. The mighty Thor leading a Christian hymn.

I moved close to Vernon and whispered. "Look at the female faces. It's pure bliss. This man is no pedophile. It's the kids' mothers he's after."

"He's certainly aware of his own charisma." Vernon winked back and nodded. We continued to sing along with the hymn.

Jensen used the gourd display as a takeoff point on his sermon about abundance and gratitude for the good things. He said nothing controversial and ended with outstretched arms that blessed everyone there. His lesson was nothing new, not to me and probably not to anyone there. He was the attraction, the reason his little church was filled.

"What you want to bet this congregation will build him a pretty manse to replace that trailer," I said to Vernon. We waited until the students left their pew and followed them.

"Wonder why Olivia isn't here," said Vernon. He had scanned the congregation several times during the service.

"She's already got a key to the door," I said.

Jensen stood at the exit, still in his robe, and shook hands with everyone. He used two hands with the ladies. When it came my turn, he grasped my elbow first and then engulfed my hand into his. "It's nice of you to come," he said, his head slightly bowed and his eyes fixed on me. I was supposed to swoon about then, but I nodded and smiled instead.

Vernon and I walked away. He was in a hurry to make sure the students got into their van and didn't linger in the scene area. They were talking when we reached them.

"Okay, what are you guys really doing out here?" he asked.

Carl turned and faced the van, while both girls stiffened.

"Reena?"

She wasn't able to stay quiet. "It's Dalton," she said. "We haven't seen him and we thought he might have come out here."

"I see." Vernon looked at them for a moment. "Let us do the searching, okay?"

"It's kind of hard to just sit and wait," said Lily.

"It's best," said Vernon, "but in case you'd like to have something to do, meet me at the Candlestick Mortuary tomorrow at three. You'll all be out of class by then, right?"

Three faces froze.

"We have to?" said Lily.

"Unless you want a court order to do so," said Vernon. I glanced at him, knowing he really couldn't force this meeting.

Reena rested against the side of the van, her cane held loosely in one hand. "We have to," she said in a quiet voice.

They left in the van.

"Will they show up?" I asked.

"Most likely," Vernon said, and they're hiding something. "Guilt danced all over their faces."

His phone rang.

"Some fishermen have found a sunken boat. Tony wants us suited up now."

We chewed on peanut butter crackers and drank sodas after we grabbed my scuba gear and headed for the county bridge that ran across Palmetto River near the entrance to the brackish water. This river lane led out to the bay and finally to the Gulf of Mexico.

The waters were warmer here, and manatees swam about, often running into motor blades.

The department hummer took us around the edge of the river to the point where fisherman had located the boat.

Edging off the bank, we landed in deep water and a current that wanted to sweep us out to sea. It was clear here, and not far to the wreckage. We swam around the boat first to check for anything that might harm us, then closed in to find a bottom full of long, choppy slices. It was like a devil had got hold of a sickle, and in a fit of fury, massacred the boat. We looked inside as best we could from one side. When the boat took on water, it listed and sank to the bottom on its other side. No one was there, but we did get the registration number from the side of the hull.

"You'll have to pull it up to see if anything is jammed beneath," I said. I sat on the bank, sipping a soda. Vernon stashed the gear in the hummer.

Before Tony could find something else for us to do on a Sunday afternoon, his phone rang. It was the deputy on boat patrol, and he was just beyond the bridge where the water opened up to the Gulf.

"He's got a small, untethered boat shoved onto the beach," he said. "And it's got Serpent Sally written on the side."

"Edwin's!" I climbed into the department boat with Tony and Vernon for the short ride to the Gulf.

"I tried to start it," said the deputy who had found it, "but it's out of gas."

I wanted to laugh. Edwin never bought much gas at one time, and when he did, it was in a can that he poured into the tank when he needed it. A thief got outsmarted by the village dummy this time.

"Doesn't seem to be damaged," said Vernon as he skirted the

boat with its peeling paint. "Better get the print guys out here."

Things began to move quickly. Tony got the report on the sunken boat in a phone call.

"It's registered to a Dalton Paige. That's the college kid we've got under surveillance for some reason." Tony glared at me but demanded no explanation.

"And I'll bet you'll find his prints on Edwin's boat," I said. "He wrecks his and tries to steal another, first mine, then Edwin's."

"But how did he get back where you were after wrecking his all the way up here?" said Vernon.

"Other stolen boats? Walked? You won't know until you find him."

Late on a Sunday night, a crane finally pulled Dalton's boat from the water. There was no sign of him other than one wet blanket and an empty fried chicken box.

"You know," I said to Vernon as we lay between the sheets, too tired to even turn toward each other, "that car that Edwin keeps hearing in the woods. Could Dalton have driven it into that thick brush?"

"You want me to get up, don't you?" Vernon didn't say another word but called Tony about the car noise and that someone should check it. "Can you believe he wanted me to do it?"

"You're not going, are you?"

"Not on your life. Loman is on duty."

I smiled at poor old Loman traipsing about nettles and moldy leaves and tree trunks in the dark, looking for a car where one shouldn't be.

Morning came early, too early, and I found myself headed for campus sooner than usual. Vernon had trotted off with his coffee to a place in the woods, because Loman had surprised everyone and located car tracks. Following them with his flashlight, he came upon a red sports car stuck in deep mud, its underpinnings probably wrecked by driving over bushes.

"And it's registered to Dalton Paige," he said as he closed his phone. "We need to find that guy."

On campus, I waited near the kiosk where Reena bought her coffee. She came alone, limping with her cane. I handed her the cup I'd already bought for her.

"I'm not well this morning," she said.

"Sit down, Reena. No one feels much like Pollyanna right now."

We sat at a small table away from the early students, who appeared to be recuperating from wild weekends. The air was brisk and the coffee hot.

"You'll show up at the mortuary today, right?"

She stared at me, her eyes watering. "I'm not sure if I can, Miz Fogarty. It's all so awful."

"What is?"

She looked away. "I don't want to tell anything second-hand. You need to hear it from Carl, really."

"Where's Dalton?" I asked.

She turned back to me, her tears beginning to slide down her cheeks. "We don't know, and I'm telling you on the level. We just don't know."

"Are you sure Lily and Carl will show up today?"

She shook her head. "Carl wants to run, but I don't think he will. Lily won't let him." She glanced at me, fear showing through the tears. "I don't want to be with them, Miz Fogarty, but I can't drive yet."

"You can ride with me right from here," I said. "Meet me at this table before three.

She seemed grateful although I could hear her gasp a few sobs as I walked away.

After lunch, I phoned Vernon to tell him I'd bring Reena.

"Good. I'll drive by that building and make sure the other two get there." I heard him turn to someone in the office and come back to the phone. "Just thought you'd like to know. The car is definitely Dalton's and it looks like he was living in it a few nights. Food all over the place, blankets and pillows, and tons of morgue comic books."

"Morgue comics? Not space ones?"

"Morgue. Creepy stuff."

I sighed. We were going to hear a whale of a story at three.

Tony had warned Mr. Wise and his assistant to be ready for the meeting in his office. Wise was not at all happy. He said he had a funeral the next day and would have to work all night if he took time off for the sheriff.

"Then work all night," Tony had told him.

Reena was at the table and ready to go when I arrived at quarter to three. There were no signs of tears.

"I'm ready, Miz Fogarty. I'm scared but I'm ready."

In the car, I tried to ease her a bit by asking how the four had met.

"We've known each other for a long time, from high school. We ended up in some of the basic courses together when we first came here and just stayed friends." She looked out the window. "I doubt now that was a good idea."

"Not too late to change your friends," I said. She didn't answer.

Wise took us to an empty viewing room where he had placed seating for all of us. It still looked like mortuary decor, and Reena and I sat like stiffs on the straight back chairs until Vernon came through the door. Lily and Carl were with him, frowning. Carl's hands were shaking, and he kept shoving them into his tight jeans pockets.

Vernon sat us around a table Wise had added to try and make it seem like a conference room. Tony and Loman were the last to enter. When they closed the door, it was like a lid on a coffin, and the college kids deflated as though death had grabbed their souls.

"This is not an official interrogation as of now," said Tony. "First, I want to know, Mr. Wise, who were the kids who worked in this place."

Wise darted his eyes at the students, at his assistant, and back again. "All three and one other, as I recall."

"But I thought you hired mortuary trainees only," I said. "Carl and Reena are in anthropology."

Wise shrugged. "We took their word for it. I mean, really, how many people would lie about that, and if they did, why?"

"Why indeed," I said and stared at Reena.

She shifted as though her leg hurt and made a tiny grunt sound. "I was here for only a week. I didn't like it much."

"And you two?" asked Tony.

Carl looked at his feet and mumbled. "Three months, in the summer."

"Me too," said Lily and joined Carl in staring at the floor.

"And Dalton?" I asked.

"He was here the longest," said Carl. "This was going to be his field, or at least the forensics part. He said this was great training."

"What duties did you have?" asked Loman whose frown questioned why anyone would want to prepare bodies for burial.

"We lifted the bodies after they were prepared and put them inside the coffins. Sealed the coffins and escorted them to the cemetery."

"Did you ever open them for viewing?" asked Vernon.

"If that was requested, yes," said Reena. "I hated doing that and I quit when I'd seen one dead person too many."

Tony stood up and paced the dark room. One end had curtains for walls. He shoved them aside to reveal storage shelves. "Did any of you ever handle funerals where you knew there would be no open casket?"

All three nodded.

Tony took in a deep breath and faced them. "Did any one of you ever remove a body before it was buried?"

Carl and Lily aimed their eyes for the floor again, but Reena's filled with tears. She sobbed openly, blubbering on her shirt.

"He said it would be fun!" She nearly yelled.

Wise nearly rose off his chair. His assistant paled.

"Who said?" asked Tony.

"Dalton! Damn him! Dalton!"

CHAPTER TWENTY-THREE

All of us were shaking in the cool mortuary viewing room by the time Reena got through her tale. It was a case of student prank gone wild and crazy—at least that's what we thought.

"Dalton got us to come and work here and help him steal the bodies. It was only three old people," said Carl as though low numbers and high age would ease the shock.

Wise gasped. "This will ruin us." He leaned toward his assistant and she nodded.

"Three elderly people?" asked Vernon.

Carl nodded. "They were old and didn't look too good. The family didn't want to see them, I guess."

"Not everyone wants the public to see their loved ones dead," I said.

Carl stayed silent, but Lily spoke up finally.

"It wasn't kicks. I mean we didn't really enjoy it. Dalton was the one getting the kicks."

"Who did the sawing?"

Reena burst into terrible sobs at this. She showed signs of vomiting, but it turned out to be only gagging. The assistant handed her a box of tissues.

"Dalton did all that," said Lily. "He wanted to practice, he said. And he found the alligator."

Stunned silence permeated the place. Even Reena made an

attempt to stifle her tears.

"I'm going to terminate this meeting now," said Tony. "All of you will accompany me to the sheriff's department where you'll be interrogated on tape. If you've got lawyers, call them."

The meeting ended. I turned to Vernon. "What now?"

"This is going to be the easiest search warrant we've ever gotten," he said.

Loman was on the phone already. By evening, they would be in Dalton's house.

Vernon called when they had the warrant. They weren't going to wait for daylight. I couldn't be part of the search, but I was welcome to sit in the car at curbside and wait for the outcome. If they needed me for anything, I'd be available. With no water holes to dive in here, Vernon was just making sure I wasn't left out of the process.

Halogen lights and white suited men swarmed beyond the trees and into the tiny house. Dalton wasn't there, and since his car had been found, we wondered where he was spending the night. At one point, Marshall Long returned to the scene wagon with some bags. He came near where I was standing.

"Geez, Luanne. We found some stinky sludge in a barrel out back. Wonder where that came from?"

"Just test it, big man."

By eleven, people from the apartment building had lined the sidewalk across the street. Uniformed deputies kept them from the search area. I watched the crowd for signs of Dalton himself. In the beginning, flashes went off repeatedly inside the house. Hundreds of photos would later show the evidence in its natural location—natural to Dalton Paige. Following that, scene techs began bringing out bags. Across the street, we could hear hushed questions about somebody being murdered.

"Put on some shoe covers, Luanne. And gloves and a suit. Tony wants you to see this." Vernon handed me the outfit kit.

"He does?"

"Says you were the one who said we ought to watch this place. He might be feeling a little guilt. Take advantage of it."

I suited up and followed him inside. Even with the door open, the putrid smell hit me hard.

"Is someone dead in here?"

"Not now," he said.

I stood in the living room. Not one inch of the natural wall showed through. Dalton had photographed tons of dead people in coffins, body parts, and various scenes of funerals. I found the one for Preacher Billy. He had to be the one on the sidelines that day, the camera man who ran into the woods.

"It's a fascination with death," I said.

"It gets better," Vernon said and pulled me into the kitchen.

Marshall Long was holding court here. Tony, his head, hands, body, and feet covered in plastic, listened.

"This guy got hold of some morgue equipment somewhere. It's not new, but it still works." He held up a saw, the kind with the round bit used to cut into bone on an autopsy table. "And this piece of metal," he patted the top of a contraption that no cook ever saw. "This is to boil off flesh when we need to examine only the bone. Looks like he had to put it back together but he was actually using it. There are traces of flesh inside still." He raised the lid, and we all turned away. "In the ME's lab, they'd remove the flesh into special bags and burn it according to strict rules." He paused. "This guy hauled it out back and dumped it in a metal barrel with leaves. Tried to burn it." He smiled and closed the lid of the boiler. "At least until he found the alligator a more efficient receptacle." He patted the top of the lid.

"More from this kid!" Marshall edged his big hips toward a cabinet over the sink. It was long rather than tall. "Ta-da!" He opened it to three skulls grinning down at us. Two had teeth, the third had a false set propped inside. The skull caps were visibly absent.

"He took the caps off with the saw, boiled off the flesh and used them for candy bowls." Marshall raised on tiptoe and tilted one skull toward us. "Chocolate kisses in this one. Strawberry suckers in the middle one, and mints for your breath in the third." He replaced the skull and stood looking at them. "I could do this in my office," he said. "Give the place some class and a theme."

The joking only mildly covered the shock. This kid with thick glasses had actually readied real bodies for use as decor in his house. I closed my eyes and thought of the other three. Did Dalton have no conscience, and why would the others go along with him?

"I hate to ask," I said, "but what's in the bedroom and bath?"

"Haven't got down to a deep search in either one yet, but the bathroom has chemical bottles under the sink. Doubt the kid took a lot of bubble soaks in the tub, unless he climbed in with..."

"Okay, Marshall, we get your picture," said Tony.

"Bedroom is full of papers, clippings and such." Marshall shrugged and began bagging the skulls.

Before I could react, Loman emerged from the bedroom, his gloved hands clasping a folder.

"Kid was organized to a point," he said. "This has material copied from reports written on grave sites found in the swamps. It includes the old slave areas. The Folsom property gets mentioned here and there. And," he held up a copy of a clipping, "he even had the old newspaper story of the kid who hanged himself years ago."

I circled the room with my eyes, even looked up at the ceiling.

"The kid really did have a fascination with death."

"Question is," said Vernon, "did his three buddies know just how far he was into this stuff?"

We were about to find out. Tony waited until he had enough from the house search to set up the three for questioning. He had separated them from each other as soon as he got them to the department. All three called lawyers. He would stay up half the night, going through the material from the house, but he wanted us all at the sheriff's office at eight. That meant canceling all my classes for the day.

The next morning, we sat around the conference area for over an hour while lawyers talked to sheriffs. Tony finally came in to say they'd made a deal with Reena and her attorney. She'd tell all if she weren't charged.

"We agreed, temporarily," he said. "If we find she has lied at any step, we drop the deal." He stood up. "We're bringing her in now. The viewing room is open, but," he sighed and looked at me, "she wants you there, Luanne. Says it will make her more comfortable."

I smiled and Vernon winked. "She has talked to me some, as you know, Tony." I didn't look at him.

Inside the interrogation room, I sat between Tony and Loman. Vernon would view us through the mirror. Reena and her attorney sat on the other side of the table, a recording device close enough to capture her words.

"How did all of this start?" Tony asked to give Reena a way to begin.

"Dalton is a biology student, but he seemed more interested in the dead end of the science." She breathed deeply, closed her eyes and continued. "Lily is in that field, too, but she was normal about it; I mean, she just learned all the stuff like any other student."

"Okay, go on from Dalton's interest."

"Carl is a daredevil," she said. "He's always looking for a wild joke. When Dalton got a job in the mortuary, he got all excited. He somehow got Lily a job there, too. He used to brag about how easy it would be to pull out a body and replace it when the family wanted a closed casket service. Most likely, Carl liked the idea and urged him to do it." She looked at her lawyer who nodded. He had been taking notes.

"When did you go to work in the mortuary?"

"Dalton said Mr. Wise was short-handed. He told him about two friends, Carl and me, who could be hired for part-time help. It was quick. We had a summer job in no time."

"What was your duty?"

"Dalton was told to train us, because we all did the same thing. When the body had been prepared, we placed it inside the coffin, sealed it, and got it ready for the funeral or burial, whichever the family wanted. We stayed right with it until it was lowered into the ground." She shivered. "I never liked the job and only lasted a week. You'd be surprised how many people get buried in a week."

I sat rigid in the cool air conditioned room. It was difficult not to pull a Marshall joke out of the air and say "yeah, humans have this tendency to die."

"Go on," said Tony.

"Dalton showed us how to pull the body out when no one from the mortuary was looking. He had it all planned." She gulped some water in the glass that had been set before her. "He said we could open the coffin in the holding area, place the body in a bag, replace it with something heavy enough to feel like the body— Dalton was in charge of weighing the bodies, too—seal the coffin and let it go to the funeral." She sighed again and looked at her lap. "Carl used to laugh something fierce about people crying over a sack of boards, even marking its burial site with an expensive tombstone."

"Did Dalton have plans for what to do with the body once he'd pulled it out of the coffin?" I asked. Tony shot me his you're-only-a-guest look.

"Oh, yes. He said once it was in a bag, we could shove it into Carl's van and take it away. No one would ever know."

Tony made a note on a pad. "Carl owned the van?"

"Yes. Dalton has a sports car. It's not big enough to haul bodies."

"And a boat?" I asked.

"Yes. He bought one from some guy who needed cash. Got it cheap, I hear."

"Ever use the boat for the bodies?" I was pushing my luck, but it was something they needed to know.

Reena was sweating a bit now. "I only heard they might have dropped stuff in the Gulf—way out there."

"They?" asked Tony.

She nodded. "Carl helped him, I think."

Loman squirmed in his chair. The lawyer looked up at him but said nothing.

"Getting back to the van, what would you do with the body once you'd loaded it?"

"It was all just talk at first. Lily and I didn't know this, but Dalton and Carl had been checking out cemeteries and graves all over the north Florida area. Carl finally said one day how fun it would be to spread bones in various places where people came through once in a while. He said it would freak them out, and we'd have a good laugh." Reena grabbed hold of her cane that leaned against the table. "I didn't laugh very long," she said, her face angry.

"And you did this—took the bodies from the coffin?" Tony glanced at the cane and back at Loman like it was a potential weapon.

"I helped with the first one, but it was just too awful. That tiny old woman and all those smells—not decaying yet, but something medicinal. I quit working at the place."

"But Lily, Carl, and Dalton continued?" I asked.

"Yes, until the end of September. Mr. Wise said business had slacked off and he'd call them back when he needed them. He thought they'd done a terrific job." She drew in a small laugh. "He didn't have a clue about what they'd done with three bodies."

"You had something to do with spreading the bones, right?" Tony stared at her, his black eyes boring into hers.

"One day, Carl said he'd pick me up after class and we'd go spread bones. I didn't want to ask what bones. I figured they'd somehow gotten them from the mortuary but I didn't ask how. The four of us went out at night to some grave sites and kind of, well, sprinkled bones about. We did more in the area around Reverend Jensen's church because Dalton had learned about the Folsom Walking Tours. Dalton would dig around some of the graves and Carl would drop the bones inside the holes and cover them up again. We thought we heard somebody coming one time, and just tossed the rest of the bones in the pond. But," she stopped and began to laugh a little, "the skull caps floated." Her laugh turned to tears. "Carl thought it terribly funny and said let them ride the waves, but Dalton fished them out with a stick. He leaned over the bank, stuck his arms in the water and shoved them into the dirt there."

"And how did you end up in a hole that you knew was already there?" I asked.

"I didn't realize there wasn't time to refill it when we had to get out quickly. The plan was that Lily and I would walk back there and find some bones we carried in our purses." She looked at her lawyer who gave a hesitant sigh and nodded. "I was too nervous about what we were going to do and didn't watch my step." Her body crumpled into the chair, as though telling the truth were tiring.

"Did you have any idea how the bones were removed from the bodies?" Tony asked.

Reena shook her head. "I figured Dalton had found a way, but I didn't want to know. I kept telling myself the bones were already out when he and Carl got hold of them."

"And Lily?" I asked.

"Yeah, her, too." Reena rapidly nodded her head.

"All great fun, right?" Tony's jaw was working now, his anger beginning to surface.

"That's all for now," said her lawyer. He nodded toward the recorder.

Tony spoke into the recorder and shut it down. "Sir, this is not over because we have some questions about a man who was murdered later."

Before the lawyer could answer, Reena began shaking her head. "I had nothing to do with that!"

"But maybe you knew about it?" Tony turned to the lawyer. "Deal is all off if we don't get a statement on everything."

The man whispered to Reena, and she whispered back. He gave the nod and Tony pushed the button.

"What do you know about the murder of the man known as Preacher Billy Buchanan?"

Reena looked at me for a moment. "We heard about the other grave site. Or at least we overheard that lady talking to Preacher

Billy about it at the fish fry at Halloween. Dalton got all excited about there being an undiscovered slave burial site. I'd had enough and didn't go there with them. In fact, Lily had had enough, too. We sat in the van while Carl and Dalton went romping through the woods. It seemed they were in there forever, but when they came out, they were running. Dalton was mad and yelling 'shit' at everything. Carl was laughing so hard he could barely stand up."

"Laughing at what?"

"He said they'd been surprised by a black man. At first, it scared Dalton. He thought it was a ghost or maybe a caretaker. Carl," Reena hesitated and looked fearfully at Tony, "came up behind him with a stone. Then they ran."

"Did he hit him with the stone?"

Reena uttered softly, "He said he did."

"Any idea where that stone is now?" asked Loman.

"They chunked something in the back of the van. I didn't look."

The recorder had its fill and Tony shut it down again. He would let Reena go but with assurance she'd stay in her apartment.

When she and her lawyer had gone, Vernon joined us in the room.

"Seems," he said, "we've got some immature pranksters led by a nutter with a strange case of necrophilia."

Vernon had to remain in the office for the rest of the day. He would be the one to charge Carl with murder.

I headed home to take advantage of a real day off and to try and let the aberrations seep out of my skin. On the way, I phoned Pasquin. Rocking on the porch in the autumn sunshine was just what I needed.

CHAPTER TWENTY-FOUR

The critters in the woods sang out loud, reminding me of the living and that even with death, others would come to liven up the place. I rocked and let a sun ray shine on my back. Pasquin had arrived before I did, let himself inside, and had tea made. Somehow this old man knew I needed a lift and he was prepared to be part of it. But, I knew he needed the tales from the day, and he wasted no time prodding me for details.

"You planning on telling Edwin all this?" I asked.

"No. He'll find out when there's a trial. I'm just glad most of the kids are behind bars." He fanned himself with his hat and frowned. "Kinda worried about this Dalton kid. He's still out there, I guess."

"He tried to steal at least two boats after wrecking his own. Lived in his car some. That's what Edwin heard."

"They find much in his house?"

I looked at Pasquin and smiled. He needed to hear and I needed to talk. I told him everything, right down to the flesh boiler and the candy jar skulls.

"How does someone live with all that death around them?" I asked. "I've heard theories of control and such. But these weren't murder victims. They were bodies, dead and embalmed. I mean, it's like Dalton wanted someone else, natural causes in this case, to do the killing for him, but he was the one to enjoy it."

"Seems to me somebody with a fascination for funeral homes and bodies might like to join them. Think this Dalton kid lies down in a coffin, folds his arms, and pretends to die?"

"And rise again like a vampire?" I laughed. It wasn't a happy laugh. If they ever caught him, reporters and psychiatrists would compete to find out how his background led him to this point.

"Tell me," said Pasquin, his hat resting on his knee, "how different is it for one of them science lab people who work with Marshall Long to deal with boiling off flesh and for this kid to do it for his own purposes?"

I had no sure answer for this. "Perhaps it's the state of mind. Maybe the lab techs look at it as a specimen, a tool that will tell them more about the living. Dalton was playing with the dead, enjoying it, maybe more than we know."

"And the techs don't enjoy it?" Pasquin rocked his chair, making rhythms on the wood floor.

I looked at him and shrugged. "Not in the same way. It's more like job satisfaction."

He leaned back in his chair and closed his eyes. His lips began to twitch and a chuckle rose from his throat. "Best not to have a bunch of white coats standing around with their hands in their pants."

Our laughter felt good and frightened the critters. Everything went quiet except an old man and a fortyish woman who kept up the morbid jokes until we had spilled tea from our glasses.

Night brought much cooler weather. Pasquin had walked home hours ago, and Plato lay on his pillow near the fireplace. I tried to sleep, but an oak branch that needed trimming scraped against the roof just above my bedroom. My hot shower hadn't washed away the image of boiled flesh and morgue saws. At one point, I wondered if the bone Dalton sawed had sprayed tiny particles in the air and he breathed them into this lungs. Could that give you cancer like asbestos, I asked myself. The limb scraped again, and I sat up to jot a note to myself to call some tree trimmers out here.

I lay down again. "Dalton is out there somewhere. He's found a shed or some kind of shelter." There were all kinds of places— abandoned trailers, old lean-to's, even abandoned cars—that some- one could find to stay out of the weather. But he'd have to travel into heavy swamp growth and risk falling into sinkholes along with dodging snakes. Dalton, with his thick glasses, didn't appear to be the type to live such a rugged life. This thought brought to mind Pasquin's comment about such a person might want to join the dead. And the tree limb scraped again.

I sat straight up, my heart pounding. People talked about fe- males having premonitions like this, but I felt like some cold spirit had just moved across me and planted a thought in my head.

I pulled on jeans and a heavy sweatshirt along with boots. Grabbing a flashlight and poking my gun and cell phone in the pocket of a heavy jacket, I nearly leaped downstairs.

"Come on, Plato. We need to go for a ride." These magic words made the dog jump to his feet and give me competition for get- ting out the door.

I drove as fast as I dared, which was pretty fast given the hour of the night, and turned down the paved road toward Reverend Jensen's church. It seemed the stretch of road took forever, but finally I pulled under an oak just past the church.

"Now, don't bark, please," I said to Plato, who ignored me but kept quiet. He darted into the church yard first. He'd follow me, I was sure. Even if he was a wild swamp dog, he tended toward being protective.

Glancing toward Jensen's trailer, I could see no lights, and I was too far away to trigger any sensors. I turned my back and

walked through the white cemetery to the edge of the woods. My
light made my path, and nothing else, clear. The leaves under my
boots cracked with their fall dryness. It hadn't rained for several
days.

I passed the pond. When I flashed the light that way, I picked
up the scene tape now lying flat on the ground and no longer
needed to keep people away. Tony had his culprits and all the
evidence he needed.

Pushing into the trees, I shined the light around the graves
until I reached the old trunk, Folsom's resting place, and maybe
where the ghost of a suicide still roamed at a certain hour. I could
hear a strange movement in the trees and knew what it was before
my light hit it.

Dalton Paige, a rope around his neck, swayed a few feet above
ground on a branch that had grown long and heavy over the years.
It was like it had replaced the one the kid had used years ago. It
would have been easy to climb into the oak, throw one end of the
rope around the limb and the other around your neck, and jump.
I let the light go from Dalton's body, down the tree trunk and to
the ground. The tree's roots were old and large, bulging outward
for several feet. My light hit an object between two of these roots.

Moving closer, I realized it was a stone with dark stains on it,
sitting atop a piece of paper torn from a student's notebook. I
didn't touch it but stooped to read it.

I know I can't get out of this any other way. Dalton Paige.

It was written in large felt pen.

I looked behind me. Plato's coarse hair stood up on his back,
and he sniffed the air. In the distance, we heard a sound like a
slam, and he took off in that direction, barking as though he had
to keep out the devil.

I pulled the phone from my pocket and made the call as I

walked toward Plato's barking. In a matter of moments, this dark forest would be lit up again in the glare of halogens.

"Plato!" I called him back from his stance in the cemetary. He kept a robe-clad Jensen at bay.

"I thought I heard a car," said Jensen, his hair unruly. "What are you doing out here?" He hugged himself in the cold.

"It's not going to be only me. In a few minutes, the entire sheriff's department will descend on this place. I suggest you get dressed." I'd swear I heard him say "damn!" as he turned back to the trailer.

They took him down around dawn. His dirty clothes told of his nights in the wild, and later they found he'd actually spent at least one night underneath the church. He'd had to pull away some siding to get there, and the threat of snakes and spiders would have been ever present. I couldn't help but think how like that was to being in a grave.

Later, as I stood and watched from the edge of the woods, the halogens gave off a light like moonbeams from the ground. In the tall trees in the distance, the black birds sat, unmoving, as though waiting for something.

After a fitful sleep, I welcomed the presence of two living beings to the house. We talked about Dalton, never understanding him.

"Maybe he likes them things," said Edwin as he sat next to Pasquin on my front porch. He seemed amazed at Dalton's night beneath the church. "I don't mind 'em. Stay real still and they won't hurt much. Black widows might, but you got to stay real still." He nodded at his own advice and rocked.

"That kid didn't like living things, Edwin. Now he might like your skinned snakes." Pasquin stopped a moment. "Too bad you didn't offer him a snake skin belt. He would have enjoyed that."

"And a snake skull salt shaker," I said. It was supposed to be sarcasm but Edwin had no capacity for that.

"Hey! I never made one of those." Edwin stopped rocking and sat in a suspended move to rise out of the chair.

"Now you stop all that!" said Pasquin. "We can't go inside your house and find dead things all over the place."

"I don't skin people," said Edwin and resumed his rock. "Besides, a salt shaker wouldn't work with a snake skull. Too many holes for the salt to fall through. I'd have to work in some plastic glue. Nope." He relaxed and held his glass for more iced tea.

"Mama's Table is closed for a while," said Pasquin. "She's having her knee done in a few days."

"Tulia didn't want to keep it open?"

"It's like this, my dear. Close the place and keep up your good reputation, or keep it open and let Tulia ruin it for good."

I nodded. "Nothing like the real thing."

The three of us rested in the dying sun. While both men dozed, I watched the sunset over the river with an assurance I'd see it rise from the other direction tomorrow.

CHAPTER TWENTY-FIVE

Vernon met me for dinner at a small, expensive cafe not far from campus. It catered to the downtown state workers, and from the prices, more to legislators and lobbyists. The case had almost wrapped up, or at least it was ready for the courts to take over.

"I had to watch the disinternments," he said. "Wise nearly burst a vessel when they found just what Reena had mentioned—boards instead of bodies. Dalton found a way to tie slats together and wrap them in batting so they wouldn't roll around or make noise when the pallbearers lifted the casket."

"Did you find any more body parts in the woods behind his house?" There had been the question of the other bones, from the torsos mainly. None had been at the sites or inside Dalton's house.

"Speculation is that he took them out on the Gulf and dumped them. Removing that flesh would have overwhelmed his boiler."

"How are the other two?"

"Carl hasn't talked yet. He's normally a loud mouth and joker, the kind of personality that wants to tell it all, but his lawyer has told him to say nothing. He's facing a murder charge."

"And Lily?"

"She's gone kind of strange. Has fits of shaking and crying, but instead of getting it out of her system by confessing, she holds it in. Turns downright defiant anytime we try to talk to her.

245

Her lawyer may be looking at an insanity defense. Or maybe she won't go to trial at all if she keeps it up. Judge may find her unable to cope."

I looked at a menu. "I wonder how many people at the other tables have conversations like this."

Vernon laughed quietly.

"Four kids sure ruined their futures," he said and lifted his glass of water and touched mine filled with wine. "Maybe Reena will live this down one day, but not soon."

"Like Pasquin says, makes you wonder how people get in so deep."

"Speaking of Pasquin, his buddy is up for a civic award."

"His buddy? You mean Edwin!"

"Yeah. Without his guidance to the grave site, his rousing everyone when he found Preacher Billy, the car sounds, and who can forget the hungry gator, we might not have solved this when we did."

"That's going to be quite a little ceremony," I said.

"Tell him to wear his very best snake belt."

We ate seafood prepared the French way, heavy sauces and all. It wasn't Mama's cornmeal-coated filets, but it felt like celebration anyway.

"It's not even Thanksgiving yet," I said. "Halloween went on for several days this year."

People dressed for this restaurant. Vernon had on a tie, and I had pulled out the black pantsuit again. It felt rich and alive in here; death seemed miles away.

"Ghosts will be flying out of those woods for years to come," said Vernon. He looked around the room and smiled. "Your friend, Harry, didn't have much to do after he found the fake slave stone, did he?"

I shrugged. "He concentrates on his academics now. Tony tries to use him every now and then. I think it's a guilt thing. After all, he got his injury and fear of diving on a job for Tony."

Vernon smiled again. "He's not totally concentrating on the academic subjects in his life," he nodded to his left.

A table for two near the window, a candle burning in the center, and a bucket of champagne on the side. The striking black woman sat in one chair. Her orange and brown dress draped loosely about her long, slim body. Olivia smiled across the table at her date. Harry MacAllister had on a new suit, a kind of dark affair with tiny stripes. He smiled back at her and jumped when the waiter popped the bottle.

"Here's to our ghosts and all their hauntings!" I said and raised my glass to Vernon.

Recommended Memento Mori Mysteries

Glynn Marsh Alam is a native Floridian. Born in Tallahassee, she is familiar with the live oak forests and cypress swamps of the area. She also knows the sinkholes and reptilia that abound there. She often swims in the cold, clear springs above the openings to fathomless caves. These are the settings for her Luanne Fogarty mystery series (*Deep Water Death, Dive Deep and Deadly, Cold Water Corpse, Bilge Water Bones, High Water Hellion*) and for her literary novel, *River Whispers*.

After graduating from Florida State University, Glynn worked as a decoder/translator for the National Security Agency in D.C., then moved to Los Angeles where she taught writing and literature and earned an MA in linguistics. After many years of traveling back to Florida twice a year, she has now moved there and writes full time.

Visit Glynn Marsh Alam at www.glynnmarshalam.com.